# TRISTAN VICK

# A REGOLITH PUBLICATIONS BOOK

THE LORDS OF SUMMER: INVASION
Book 2 in The Lords of Summer Series
A Dark Forces of Nature Novella
By Tristan Vick ©2025. All Rights Reserved
www.tristanvick.com

Published by Regolith Publications
First Edition, copyright © October 31, 2025.

Cover art used A.I.
Cover design by: Regolith Design
Written & Edited by Tristan Vick

# Contents

# 1

## INVASION
### PART 1: SUGAR AND SPICE

THE SKY HAD CRACKED OPEN AND IT RAINED fire and brimstone down onto the valley in every direction. Meteors the size of Mitch McIntyre's dad's Cadillac smashed into the landscape across most of North America. Billy Bardem turned up the AM/FM radio that sat on the green picnic table in his backyard, and a quiet fell over the group as we listened intently to the emergency broadcast.

A news reporter frantically urged listeners to stay inside their homes, lock their doors, and turn up all their lights. You see, the meteors had brought with them strange alien creatures from another world. Creatures that were sensitive to our wavelength of light. All this is how we knew, this was, without a doubt, going to be the weirdest summer of our lives.

After our harrowing encounter with one of the

fang-toothed, indigo glowing creatures and our epic standoff at Fort Liberty, the treehouse a half mile into the woods behind Billy Bardem's house, we counted ourselves lucky to still be alive. It was as the newsman had said on the radio, the creatures hated bright light. And we had blasted the creature with Jimmy's stash of Fourth of July fireworks—and sent it packing. But it wasn't dead. It was still out there somewhere, waiting for the night to come when it could slink out of whichever cave it had found to hide away in—and then it would start its reign of bloody terror all over again.

My sister Melody, Billy "Backwoods" Bardem, Mitch "Big Mac" McIntyre, Paul "The Brain" Anders, Jimmy "Mad Dog" Polson, the sophomore cheerleader Sarah Lewis, and myself, Travis "Maverick" Mahoney, all convened back at Billy's house after the ordeal. It was to our great surprise to find all of our parents gathered at Billy's house, preparing for the worst.

By the amount of meteors falling all around us, Billy's mom wasn't wrong when she said, "This is an invasion, kids. Best you learn some survival skills."

She nodded at Billy and he smiled and nodded back, acknowledging without so many words that it was time to get down to brass tacks. The order of the day was to get some weapons training. Paul's dad, Mr. Anders, had called in his nephew Drake, a recent police academy graduate, to show us the proper gun safety. Naturally, he oversaw our training making sure to emphasize that firearms were meant to be lethal tools and that we should only use them if the aliens were attacking us.

But before letting any of us graduate to firearm users, he said we had to read William Golding's book *Lord of the Flies*. It had something to do with learning right and wrong in a survival situation and what a delicate balance it was. Life, Drake said, was balanced on a razors edge. Learning to shoot was just a technical ability. Needless to say, other than for our self-defense training, none of us would be using guns. It wasn't like the library would be open in the midst of an alien invasion.

As for Billy, he covered all the other basic survival skills such as tying knots, starting fires with nothing but two sticks and some twine, and how to properly wrap a wound. You know, all the basic things he had learned in the Boy Scouts.

Meanwhile, Billy's mom, Caroline, taught us

foraging, what kinds of berries and mushrooms were safe to eat, and she also showed us how to gut a fish. She informed us that small game such as squirrels or a rabbits wouldn't be much different and then she slapped a raw fish down on the table to have us try. The disgusted look on Melody's face was priceless.

My mother, Emily, showed us how to make a basket weave from straw or grass, and how to sew a basic stitch, just in case we ran into another situation where we needed to stitch something up. Hopefully not a person. But as Melody had shown us when she'd stitched Sarah's wounds up that night the alien attacked us, it was a skill worth having.

Our parents had laid all the groundwork to mount a resistance, and after a long day of hard work and thorough preparation, we barbequed hot dogs and burgers.

"Eat up," my mom said. "We don't know what tomorrow holds or, for that matter, if there will be more of those things on the loose. But y'all have been through it, and you need to keep your strength up."

I nodded and looked over at Billy who also nodded in agreement. We all helped ourselves to seconds while Paul and Mitch had thirds. When I looked over at my sister, I saw Melody yawn, her eyes heavy with exhaustion. My mom went over to her and, taking her by the hand, guided her into Billy's house. Pausing in the back entrance, she glanced back, and said, "Travis, tell your friends goodbye. We're staying the night with the Bardem's. You'll be able to meet up again tomorrow once everyone has had a time to rest."

"Sleepover!" I said, excitedly, and Billy and I fist-bumped.

"Ah, man," Paul said. "I want to stay too."

"Me too," Mitch added.

They both looked toward Billy who turned to his mom. "Can they stay, mom?"

Carol laughed. "It's fine by me. You can all stay. But you must ask your parents first."

"Yes," Mitch said triumphantly, under his breath.

Both the Anders and McIntyres nodded in the affirmative and Mitch's dad added, "It's fine by us."

"What about you, Jimmy?" I asked, noticing he was the only one not excited about staying over.

"I wish I could. But I gotta get home and check on my mom. She's all by herself."

"Come on, kid," Mr. McIntyre said, putting his

hand on Jimmy's shoulder. "I'll give you a ride."

"Thanks, Mr. McIntyre. I appreciate that," Jimmy answered. He sounded humbler and more mature than we'd ever heard him. But, for him, his mom was his whole world and we all sense the worry in his voice.

We said our goodbyes to Jimmy and the other parents, including the Kims, the McIntyres, the Anders, and even Drake and his two Rottweilers, Rocky and Bullwinkle.

"Stay safe!" I said, waving goodbye.

When I turned back around I saw Sarah Lewis walk up to Billy's mom. "Mrs. Bardem, is it all right if I use your phone? I want to call my parents and let them know I'm okay."

"Of course, dear. It's just in the kitchen there." Billy's mom jutted her chin toward the back door of the house since it lead into the kitchen and Sarah nodded and quickly went inside and began dialing the sand-colored rotary phone that hung on the wall next to the refrigerator.

While mom put Melody to sleep, Billy and I helped his mother set up the flood lights in the backyard. If that thing came back this way, the lights would be powerful enough to give it scorching burns, especially since we now knew that it's skin reacted badly to infrared light.

Carol and my mom, whose first name was Emily, stayed up into the wee hours of the morning chatting and drinking coffee and tea. The kept all the houselights on, to help dissuade any aliens from encroaching on our surroundings. Like a couple of loving hens, they kept watch throughout the night while the rest of us got ready to sleep in the basement den.

As I walked down the hall, from Billy's bedroom, I found Mitch and Paul crouched down in front of the bathroom door. They were trying to peer through the keyhole.

I looked past them to see Sarah come around the corner wearing red plaid pajamas as she dried her hair with a towel. Our eyes met and we both looked at Mitch and Paul and then back at each other. I shrugged and Sarah held a finger up to her lips to let me know to keep her presence a secret.

Drawing up close to Mitch and Paul, I leaned over their shoulders and whispered, "What are we looking at?"

"Shhh…" Mitch hushed, "Sarah's getting out of the shower."

"Don't be a perv," I said.

"Don't be a buzzkill," Paul shot back.

"You know," Sarah said, inching up next to me as we stood behind Mitch and Paul, "I heard she had a tattoo of a phoenix right on the small of her back."

"How do you know that?" asked Paul turning his head to find Sarah's grinning face hovering right next to his. He gulped hard when the realization set in. "Oh, crap on a stick."

"Shut up you guys, I think I see some movement."

Paul began to shake Mitch's shoulder, his eyes still glued to Sarah's. "Hey, dude."

"What?"

"Dude."

"Stop shaking me, I can't see…" Mitch stopped mid-sentence when he looked over to find Sarah standing beside him.

"I tried to tell you," Paul said.

"We, uh, were just…"

"Being a couple of pervs," I said.

"Yeah," Paul said apologetically, "Sorry about that."

Sarah stood up and laughed. "No harm, no foul," she said. Then the toilet flushed and we all jumped back from the door.

The bathroom door swung wide open and Billy stood there looking at us, a puzzled look on his face. "Um… hi, guys. What's going on?"

"You idiot!" Paul said slapping the back of Mitch's head.

"Ow," Mitch groused, as he rubbed his head. "What was that for?"

"Do you realize we almost saw more of Billy than we cared to see?"

"I don't follow," Mitch said, still not getting it.

"Guys," Billy said, talking over their bickering to try and get their attention. "Guys, you're blocking the exit."

"Come on," I said, gesturing for them to follow me. "I laid out the sleeping bags."

"Wait, why is Sarah still here?" Mitch asked, looking at us then Sarah, then back at us again.

"I talked to my parents on the phone," Sarah informed us, "and two meteors have crashed down on the other side of town near where I live. The police and national guard have set up quarantine zones around the crash sites. Since I can't get home, Carol suggested I spend the night here with everyone."

"She can sleep on the couch with me," a small voice said and we all turned to find Melody standing behind us.

Sarah walked over and took her hand and they strode happily out into the den. We all shared glances and then, with nothing more to be said, we followed suit.

Our sleeping bags were lined up, side-by-side, in the middle of the floor. The sofa was made up like a bed, and reserved for Sarah. Melody climbed onto the couch with Sarah and they snuggled up together. Meanwhile, Mitch and Paul's sleeping bags were next to each other while Billy's was next to mine.

"Sarah," Billy said. She raised her head and propped it up with her hand, as she rested her elbow behind Melody's head. She batted her eyes at him and waited for him to finish what he had to say. "You can sleep in my room, if you want."

"I'm fine right here," she said, her smile growing even brighter. "Besides, we've stuck together this far… all of us… and I think we should stay together. Especially if that thing comes back."

"Do you think it'll come back," asked Mitch, his voice cracking as he gulped nervously.

"Maybe," Sarah replied. "I don't know. We don't know how intelligent it is. Like, is it smart like a dog or does it have human level intelligence? We don't know if it's just acting on instinct or if it has actual motives and plans."

"What kind of plans?" I asked. "I mean, considering it's not of this world. What kind of plans would an alien invader even have?"

"World domination," Paul answered. We all looked at him.

"World domination?" Billy asked. "How do you figure?"

"Have any of you ever heard about the Fermi Paradox?"

We collectively shook our heads, no. Paul nodded, pushed up his classes, and continued to educate us.

"A physicist named Enrico Fermi hypothesized that given the sheer amount of galaxies, stars, and planets that we can see out of our telescopes, the universe should be teaming with life."

"And yet," Sarah added, "we haven't come across

any… until now, that is."

"That's right," Paul continued. "You see, Fermi theorized that there were two possible explanations for why we hadn't seen extraterrestrial life. One was, our world was, perhaps, the very first to evolve life. And being the first, there was nobody else yet alive to contact us. However, this theory is statistically unlikely, given the sheer number of stars and planets out there, not to mention the sheer age of the universe."

"Why do I have a bad feeling about his second theory?" Mitch sat crisscross apple sauce on his sleeping bag and listened intently to Paul's micro lecture.

"The second idea, as you might have guessed, is that we don't see any signs of alien life because they've all died off. This second hypothesis suggests that they either went extinct because of their own stupidity like suffering the consequences of nuclear war, or because they were conquered by evil aliens who sucked up all their resources."

"So, let me get this straight," I said. "After these evil aliens swoop in and strip the other worlds barren, they only leave behind the husks of once thriving worlds which are now little more than rocky corpses floating in the lifeless void of space?"

"Basically, yeah," replied Paul.

Mitch gulped. "Sometimes I hate being right. But, if what you said is true, and the second theory is what we're dealing with, then I think it's safe to say it's all much more disconcerting than any of us initially thought."

"Okay," Billy said, following Paul's train of thought. "But that still doesn't explain why you think this invasion might be to take over the planet."

"Think of it this way. Sending genetically bred murder creatures to a world on asteroids is the best way to fly under the radar, quite literally, and then release a swarm of killing machines to clear the path for the pending invaders."

"So, what are you saying?" I asked. "That there's some even more advanced alien race out there that has sicked their junkyard dogs on us?"

"I mean," Paul let out a contemplative sigh, "it's just one possibility."

"All right, everyone," Sarah said, "I think that's enough talk for the night. We've got to get some rest because tomorrow is going to be its own new challenge."

"Agreed," I said. Billy, Paul, and Mitch nodded and climbed into their sleeping bags.

"Goodnight, y'all," Sarah said. "Goodnight, Billy," she added, shooting him an especially warm smile.

"Goodnight," he replied, falling back onto his pillow and letting out a long sigh, a massive smile settling onto his face. That's the last thing I remember before falling fast asleep.

However, my sleep was short lived. A couple of hours later, in the midst of our sweet dreams, I roused awake when I heard footsteps. I cracked my eyes open to see Sarah walking toward Billy and I. Crouching down, she opened Billy's sleeping bag and tapped him on his back. "Scoot over."

"Is something wrong?" he asked, sleepily.

"Melody kicks like a mule in her sleep. I'll have the bruises to prove it. Scoot, so I can sleep here, with you."

"Oh," Billy replied. "Sure." Sarah settled into Billy's sleeping bag with him and then wrapped her arms around him, pressed her face into his neck and nuzzled the back of his head. In that moment, she reminded me of our cat, Elvis.

Billy's eyes grew large and I could tell he was nervous, but at the same time he didn't want to ruin whatever this thing was between him and Sarah. He'd never had a girlfriend before. So, he didn't know what to do.

Without even saying a word, I stretched out my arm, made a fist and held it there until Billy gave me a fist bump. It was a gesture that said, "Way to go, bro."

"Travis," Sarah's voice whispered. "I saw that."

I immediately fell back onto my pillow and began to fake snore, opening my right eye just a crack to see her smile at me in amusement.

"Just go to sleep, you dork."

As my eyelids grew heavy, I could hear the soft laughter of our mothers upstairs. They'd obviously broken open a bottle of wine and had gotten a little tipsy and were now laughing at things that weren't even funny. Which, in itself, was kind of funny.

As I drifted off to sleep, Paul's rhythmic snoring filled the room with an soothing white noise, I felt at peace for the first time in the past two days.

Sarah was right, I thought. Tomorrow was going to have its own challenges and we'd need to start preparing for the worst, because if what Paul had said was at all true, then this wasn't the real invasion. This was simply laying the ground work for the real invaders to show up and claim an already ravaged planet.

# 2

# INVASION
## PART 2: INFILTRATOR

**THE SUN WAS BEGINNING TO RISE, THE HORIZON** awash with hot pinks that bathed everything in a warm glow. "Well," Mitch said, sitting up and stretching and yawning at the same time, "we made it through the night."

"Hey," I said, looking around, "Where's Billy?" Mitch merely shrugged and Paul was still rubbing the sleep out of his eyes. We all looked over at Sarah Lewis sleeping in Billy's sleeping bag. Her plaid pajama shirt rode up on her, exposing her midriff and stomach. She had one hand resting across her chest and the other arced over her head and entangled with a mess of hair.

"Holy smokes, she's hot," Paul said, pulling off his glasses, breathing steamy breath on the lenses, and rubbing them clean with his own shirt. He put them back on and looked down at her again.

"Hey," he said, pointing at her bellybutton. "Her wounds are gone."

The three of us huddled around Sarah and we were judiciously inspecting her abdomen when her eyes cracked open to find the three of us looking at her bare stomach.

"What's going on, Trav?" she asked, sitting up.

"Your wounds," I said, lifting up the flap of her plaid flannel and looking at her stomach. "They're completely healed."

"What?" Sarah said, and pulled up her shirt to her sternum and rubbed her hand down her flat stomach. Mitch gulped, then stood up and scurried off. As he ran away, he called back over his shoulder, "I… uh… gotta go to the… um… bathroom."

Paul just shook his head. "No, he doesn't. He's just embarrassed because he's only used to seeing his sister… like this." Paul pointed at Sarah's bare stomach and waved a finger about as if to say, 'this right here.'

Sarah put her shirt down and stood up. "That's weird. It's weird, right?" She turned to me, looking for answers.

I shrugged. "Beats me. Maybe our immune

systems can fight off the alien infection?"

"Yay for science," Paul exclaimed.

I nodded. "So, what are you going to do?"

Sarah looked around. "I need to find Billy."

"Yeah, he's probably freaking out that you two slept together."

"Wait, you two slept together?" asked Paul, pushing his glasses up on the bridge of his nose.

"It wasn't like that," Sarah said, looking back over her shoulder. "We only slept in the same spot. No funny business." She turned back around to face us and added, "Billy's a true gentleman. You both could learn a thing or two from him."

"Yeah," I said, smacking Paul in his arm. "Be a gentleman."

"Hey, guys," Billy's mom's voice came from the top of the stairs. "Get dressed and get up here, asap."

"Yes, ma'am!" Mitch replied, standing in the bathroom doorway. He looked over at us and I raised my eyebrows and shook my head. None of us had any clue what was going on, but it sounded urgent.

Gathering in Billy's kitchen, we found everyone awake and looking out the back window. "What is it?" I asked. Billy stepped aside and pointed out into his backyard.

"It's the military."

Sure enough, there were half a dozen armed soldiers, wearing full gear, and decked in army green camouflage standing in Billy's back yard.

One of the soldiers had on a silver backpack with antennas and modules, and blinking lights, and was attached to what appeared to be a metal-detector of some kind.

Billy's mom, Carol, was outside talking to one of the soldiers when she nodded, shook his hand, then turned back toward the house.

"What they say?" my mom asked Carol as she stepped in through the back door, the screen door slamming shut behind her with the viciousness of a mousetrap.

"They said the entire town is under lockdown. The national guard was activated in forty-seven states, and units were dispatched to any place with a downed meteorite."

"All right," I said, stroking my chin. "So, now the military is on the scene. That's good news, right?" I looked up to half a dozen blank stares.

"I don't know, Travis," Mom answered. "I

honestly don't know."

"Of course, all of you are more than welcome to stay here as long as you'd like," Carol said. "But, right now, all we can do is wait and see."

"*Ahhh* shucks," Mitch lamented. "I hate waiting."

I glimpsed Billy and Sarah stealing glances of one another and looking away bashfully.

Just then, we all heard fully automatic gunfire coming from down the street. We all rushed to the front living room window and looked out to see three army jeeps race by. The first one had a gun turret mounted on the roll cage. A soldier stood in the back and manned the gun as he fired at something in the distance. We could only assume it was one of the aliens, if not the same one we'd run into the night before.

Billy rand to the front door and swung it open.

"No!" his mom shouted, "It's too dangerous to go outside."

But her warning went unheard because Billy was already out the door and racing across his front lawn to get a better look.

"Come on," I said, excitedly, waving for Mitch and Paul to follow me."

"Travis!" my mom shouted sternly, but letting the excitement get the better of me, I ignored her.

"You idiots are going to be the death of me," Sarah said, rolling her eyes, but she followed us out to the front lawn despite her protest.

We all dashed out into the street, where Billy was standing, and slid up next to him. We watched in awe as the jeep with the gun got launched nearly thirty feet into the air. The other two jeeps got swatted hard by one of the aliens, rolled onto their sides and skidded away.

The creature was similar to the one we'd encountered in the woods. It had the face of a velociraptor, and like our previous alien friend with six eyes, three on either side of its face, this one had four central eyes with two additional ones on either side of its oblong, banana-shaped head.

Also, like our alien, it had six slender tails that looked like bullwhips with what appeared to be glowing feathers on the ends of them. Except, as we had learned from experience, they weren't feathers, but were razor-sharp extrusions that could cut through metal just as easily as flesh.

The main difference from this beast and the one

we'd encountered in the woods was that this new one was roughly two times bigger than our creature. While the first monster was akin to a six-hundred pound grizzly bear, this one was more like a twelve-hundred pound stampeding rhino.

After its thunderous roar, it locked its gaze on us and, with a shake of its head and a couple angry snorts, began to charge.

"Oh, crap!" Paul said, darting back toward the house. We all turned to run inside, but the monster was too fast. It had already burst through the neighbors hedges and skidded to a halt on the front lawn, blocking half of us from getting inside.

It roared again, purple glowing spittle flying from its jowls. It's six-tails whipping about, the feather-like razors glowing hot pink with the rage of the beast.

"Watch out for those tails," Billy shouted, ducking as one flew over his head.

"The sun isn't hurting this one," Sarah said.

The beast whipped around, tails flailing in the air like live firehoses. It kicked and snorted and made a ruckus. Fresh bullet holes from where the soldiers had shot it oozed a purple glowing blood and it was probably as frightened as it was agitated—a dangerous combination in a wild animal, for sure.

"Get away from my kids!" Billy's mom stood in the entrance with an Ithaca 37 series pump-action shotgun. She cocked it, with a *shuh-shunk*, and aiming it at the creature, blasted off a round of buckshot.

BLAM!

The buckshot peppered the side of the alien monster and, feeling the sting, it squealed like a piglet and then bounded off.

Using one arm, Carol pumped the shotgun and let another blast erupt into the air as a warning shot, just to make sure the creature knew not to mess with mama-bear.

BLAM!

"Everyone, inside. Now," she ordered.

We all did as we were told, hurried inside, and took our seats around the kitchen table. Sarah leaned against the door frame next to the phone while Billy's mom stood in the living room talking to my mom.

"That was a close one," Mitch said, still panting heavily.

"No kidding," Paul agreed. "And is it just me, or was that one bigger than the one we fought?"

"Oh, it was definitely bigger," Sarah agreed. She

folded her arms under her chest and looked over at Billy who blushed and looked down at his feet. When he looked back up at her, she smiled at him.

It was only as things began to settle down that I glanced around the table, realizing that I hadn't seen hide or hair of Melody since last night. Perhaps more pressing still, I couldn't remember seeing her this morning.

"Mom," I said, interrupting their conversation.

"Not now, sweetie," my mom replied, holding up a finger to let me know she wasn't finished talking to Carol.

"Mom," I said, more urgently.

"Not now, Travis."

"Where's Melody?" I asked, making sure it was loud enough that everyone else would hear the question too.

Both Carol and my mom stopped talking mid-sentence and turned and did a quick headcount.

"We thought she was with you," mom said.

"I haven't seen her since last night."

"That's right, Mrs. Mahoney," Sarah said. "I fell asleep next to her, but this morning, well, I don't even remember seeing her. I guess I just assumed she was upstairs or in the bathroom or something."

"We have to find her," I said. "Everyone, fan out."

We searched Billy's house high and low and then, from the garage, Mitch shouted, "Guys! In here. I found something."

Rushing into the garage, we all stood around a big bag of Halloween candy. It had Kit-kats, Nestle Crunch, and Butterfingers. Candy was haphazardly scattered all around the floor and looked as though raccoons had gotten into it.

"Did you eat all that candy?" Paul asked, looking at Mitch suspiciously.

Mitch squinted at Paul and replied, "Ha-ha, very funny, four-eyes. No, I did not eat all this candy." He turned and looked at us and then, feeling anxious, blurted out, "Well, all right. I had one of the Butterfingers. But just one." Letting out a sigh, as though he'd been caught red-handed even though we hadn't said anything, he added, "Alright, fine, that's a lie. I had two. Maybe three pieces. But that's it. I swear!"

I bent down next to the bag of candy and pulled up one of Mom's headscarves. She reached over and grabbed it and, holding it in her hands, carefully inspected it. "Is that one of mine?"

"Yes," I said. "Melody had brought it to Fort Liberty with her."

"So, she was here," Sarah said.

"It's not like her to just steal candy," I said. "She doesn't even like candy."

"What little kid doesn't like candy?" asked Mitch. Paul smacked him in the arm to get him to shut-up. "Ow," he replied, shooting Paul a disgruntled look.

"She obviously took out her things from her bag and stuffed it full of candy." I looked up and pointed at the back door to the garage which hung open. "And then probably went that way."

We all looked out the back of the garage to see Fort Liberty looming on the crest of the distant hill that was tucked away in the woods behind Billy Bardem's house.

"If I had to make a guess, I'd bet you my mint Micky Mantle baseball card that she went back to Fort Liberty."

It was a wild guess on my part, but it was the only guess that fit all the clues. There'd be no reason for her to head home alone, not with both mom and me being here. She obviously didn't want anyone to know where she was going, so she had snuck out.

"But why would she go back there?" asked Mitch. "That thing, for all we know, is still out there."

"Why do little sisters do anything?" I asked.

"Fair point," Mitch replied.

"As for the creature," Billy said, "It's probably hiding in some cave or within the thick cover of the forest. If she doesn't go too deep into the forest, she should be okay. But we'd better go check on things, just to be sure." Billy turned to his mom and locked eyes.

After a long silence, Carol finally nodded and said, "You find that little girl, Billy. And you bring her back safe and sound."

"We all will, Mrs. Bardem," I said, nodding at Billy and then turning to my mom. Tears flooded her eyes, but she kept a brave face.

"I'd tell you not to go, what with military roaming about and the Sherrif setting a curfew and everything. But, the truth is, it's not safe anywhere right now. So, you go find your sister and bring her back. And if you see one of those things, don't play hero and get reckless. Stay smart out there."

I could tell she had more to say. She probably

wanted to tell me how much she loved me and kiss my forehead and embarrass me in front of all my friends. But instead, she just reached out, took me in her arms, and gave me the biggest hug of my life.

"I will, Mom," I answered. "I promise."

Before we could break away and head off on our grand hunt for Melody, we heard a voice from the driveway, "Hey, it seems you losers could use an extra hand."

We turned to see Mitch's sister, Megan, standing in the middle of the driveway. She had on roller-skates, knee and elbow pads, ripped jean shorts, a jersey with the number sixteen on it, a roller derby styled helmet with mesh faceguard, and held a hockey stick in her hands which she casually leaned on as she smiled at everyone.

Megan was one of the popular girls at school. She was tall. Like freakishly tall for a high school girl at five-foot-ten and she also had the biggest chest in the entire senior class, much to Mitch's chagrin since we constantly reminded him of the fact.

Although Mitch always called Megan chubby, and plain, and said she had a hairy back, having a whole repertoire of insults for his sister who perpetually annoyed him, she wasn't anything like how he depicted her. She was nearly as beautiful as Sarah Lewis, and was last year's Homecoming Queen. So, the rumor of her ugliness was greatly exaggerated.

"Megan?!" Sarah said excitedly upon catching sight of her classmate. "Megan, is that you?"

Sarah ran over to Megan and practically leaped into her arms. Megan caught her and rolled back a bit on her skates as they giggled and hugged. Holding each other's forearms, the looked into one another's eyes, laughed some more, and hopped up and down gleefully.

"I'm so happy to see you, Megs. You have no idea!"

"Same," Megan said. "I heard about what happened at Make-out Point. Truth be told, I thought you were dead."

"I'm very much alive. But…" Sarah's voice trailed off and we watched as the excitement for seeing her friend quickly turned to sadness as she reflected on the traumatic loss of her boyfriend and friends.

"What about Dean? Did he make it out alive?"

"I'm afraid he's… uh, he…" Sarah couldn't bring herself to say the words and burst into tears and, clutching Megan by her arms, she buried her face into Megan's shoulder. Megan just scanned our solemn faces and rubbed Sarah's back as she let her cry on her shoulder.

"I'm sorry," Megan said. "I can't begin to imagine what you must have gone through." Then, after a long pause, she asked, "By the way, why are you wearing my clothes?"

"Oh," Sarah said, taking a step back and looking down at herself. "I suppose I am."

"Where in the world did you find those? I haven't seen them for ages. They went missing weeks ago."

Both Sarah and Megan looked over at Mitch, who gulped hard.

"Mitch had them stowed in his Duffle bag," Sarah informed. "I don't really know why. I was just glad they were things I could wear. But I had to borrow a bra and underpants from Mrs. Bardem, since Mitch didn't have any of those."

Megan threw her hands on her hips. "Care to explain, oh brother of mine?"

Mitch gulped. "Well, you see, we sometimes stuff straw into the clothes of girls who've wronged us and then burn the effigies. So, I borrowed some of your clothes."

"You do what now with my clothes?" Megan asked, her voice spiking with bewilderment. "You're burning them? You little snot-faced pimple-popper!" Megan's face turned so bright red you'd swear steam was about to come out of her ears. Raising her hockey stick, she started skating toward Mitch who grabbed Paul, shoved him out in front, and used him as a makeshift human shield.

"Hey, man! Not cool," objected Paul. He wasn't about to be the fall guy for Mitch's idiotic beef with his sister.

Luckily, Sarah caught Megan by her shorts waistband, leaned back to anchor herself, and held Megan back. Megan thrashed around and swung her hockey stick from side to side, but was too far away to hit her annoying little brother.

"All right, ladies," Mrs. Bardem said, "We have more important things to worry about than the antics of adolescent boys. Namely, we have to—"

"What's everybody doing in the garage?" a small voice asked.

For the second time, we found ourselves pivoting back toward the door to the garage. Melody stood in the doorway, her eyes cheerful and bright as she looked at everyone, a half-smile curling onto the corner of her mouth. She looked amused, but also a little uncertain as to why everyone was gathered in the garage.

"My baby, girl!" my Mom screamed and she practically shoved me and Billy out of the way and dashed to Melody, fell to her knees, and embraced my sister who was a little perplexed by everything.

"Where on Earth did you disappear to?" My mom asked, holding Melody by her shoulders and giving her a stern look.

"I left some of my things at the fort. I wanted to get them before night time, because the monster might come back."

"Why would you do something so stupid?" I asked.

"Actually, that's pretty smart," Paul interjected. "If she'd gone at night, there's no telling what might have happened. She could have been disemboweled like Sarah's boyfriend."

"Dude!" Billy said, looking at Paul and then to Sarah.

We all looked at Sarah who's eyes brimmed with

tears. Fighting back sobs, she buried her face in her arm and turned and ran out into the yard.

"Nice going, paper-for-brains," Megan said sternly, pointing the hockey stick at Paul who raised his hands and took a step back.

Megan turned and rolled down the driveway and then stepped onto the lawn with her skates and walked over to Sarah. Throwing an arm around Sarah's shoulders, she drew her in for another comforting embrace.

"I didn't mean it like that. What I meant was…"

"It doesn't matter," Billy said. "The damage is already done." Billy turned and went in the opposite direction, squeezing past Melody and my mom, and out into the back yard.

"Come on little one," my mom said. "You come along and get washed up and then you can help me make ham and cheese sandwiches for lunch."

Mitch stood grinning at Paul with a very strange, oddly manic grin. Paul finally sighed and turned toward Mitch. "What?"

"At least she doesn't want to kill me anymore."

"Haha," Paul said sarcastically. "Very funny."

"Because she wants to kill you."

"Yeah," Paul answered. "I got that."

"Wait, do you guys hear that?" I asked. They both stopped fighting long enough to listen. "It's like some sort of high pitch whistling."

That's when we looked out of the open garage door and saw a shadowy dark object falling from the sky about three blocks away. As the object loomed close, I squinted as hard as my eyes would allow and realized what it was I was looking at.

"Get down!" I shouted, running into the yard, toward Sarah and Megan. But my words had barely time to reach their ears when the bomb exploded.

Three blocks away a massive fireball rose up, engulfing at least three additional city blocks beyond that. Luckily, the blast erupted away from us, but it kicked up a vicious shockwave that jostled the trees as it rushed toward us.

Sarah and Megan turned to me and then looked at the explosion. A hot blast of air, like an invisible tsunami, hit us and knocked all three of us off our feet and blew us back at least a couple of yards.

Everything went black, and I think that I must have been knocked unconscious, because the next thing I know Billy, Paul, and Mitch were dragging

Sarah, Megan, and I from the lawn. They pulled us back into the garage and Billy slammed the garage door shut and looked at us.

"Are you guys all right?" he asked.

I nodded and looked at Sarah, who nodded as well. Megan sat staring vacantly at the wall, still in shock.

"The military is bombing the town," Billy informed us.

"But why would they—"

Paul's question was cut short by the inside door to the kitchen flying open and slamming against the wall. Billy's mom appeared in the doorway and shouted, "Everyone, get to the basement. Now!"

# 3

## INVASION
### PART 3: BREAK 'EM OFF A PIECE OF KIT-KAT BAR

EMERGENCY VEHICLES RACED TOWARD THE flames from the demolished sections of town when we emerged from the basement. To our dismay, five city blocks were completely destroyed. Only a few houses stood a block away and beyond that, it looked like the aftermath of a level eight earthquake. Whatever the military had used, it was big. It wasn't a nuke, but it was powerful enough to level half a town.

"Why would they bomb us?" Mitch asked, his eyes tearing up. His voice quivered with fear and adrenaline. If we'd been just a block closer to the detonation, we'd all be dead. "Why wouldn't they give an evacuation signal. Why'd they kill all those people?"

Paul was pacing nervously then turned to us. "Guys, my parents. Our house was in the blast radius.

I need to go see if they're okay."

Paul turned to head home not realizing Megan was standing directly behind him. When he turned his face planted squarely in the center of her chest and he rebounded off her and looked up, embarrassed by the unintentional accident.

"It's too dangerous," she said.

"Megan is right," Carol agreed. "Emily and I will go check on Paul's parents. And then I'll drop Emily at the hospital. They're going to need all hands on deck for this. The rest of y'all, head into town and hit up the Walgreens. Look for medicine. Antibiotics, that sort of thing."

My mom walked up to me and handed me a wad of paper. "Here's a list of the names of the drugs you'll need to get and some extra money… just in case."

"Billy," his mom added, "I left some money in the recipe tin. There should be enough. But if nobody is there and the store is abandoned, just take it. We'll repay them when we can."

Billy nodded.

Carol walked over to Paul and put her hand on his shoulder. "Hey, kiddo. We'll find your parents. In the meantime, I need you to help your friends. Keep them safe."

"Yes, ma'am," Paul answered, pushing his glasses up on his nose and trying his best not to cry.

"Don't worry Mrs. Bardem," Megan said, "I'll keep these nerds safe."

"I'm sure you'll do a fine job too," with that Carol turned toward my mom and nodded and they both got in Carol's Chevy Celebrity wagon with wood paneling on the sides.

My mom wound down the window and called out to us, "If we're not back by dinner time, don't look for us. Stay hunkered down till' morning. If you kids get separated, make your way to the high school. That's the reserve emergency shelter."

"Okay, mom," Melody said and we all stood by the curbside as they drove off.

"They're just gone. In a flash." I turned to find Mitch still staring out across the swath of destruction. I put my hand on his shoulder.

"Are you okay, buddy?"

"It had to be bad, right? I mean, the government wouldn't have killed its own people if it wasn't bad, right?"

In the distance, gunfire erupted. The military was

engaging the aliens. Then, coming from a totally different section of town, there was more gunfire. We all heard the sound of planes, and looked up as a couple of A-10 Thunderbolt II 'Warthog' jets flew overhead. Their massive turbines squealed like a couple of angry banshees and I tapped Mitch's arm.

"Maybe we'd better head back inside," I said. We were all pretty nervous.

That's when I heard Melody say, "I think we should go back to Fort Liberty. If they're bombing the town, at least we'll be a safe distance away."

"It's not a bad idea," I said, patting her on her head. "But Mom gave us a mission, and I think we need to see it through. Isn't that right, Billy?"

When there was no reply we turned around to find Billy and Sarah standing in the front yard, their hands resting on one another's hips as they touched foreheads in a close embrace.

"Did I miss something?" Megan asked, looking over at me and then back at them.

"Oh, I'm pretty sure they've trauma bonded," I said.

Megan marched up to them, and grabbing Sarah by the arm, she dragged her away. She and Billy held hands as long as possible but were promptly pried apart. As Megan marched off with Sarah in tow, we could hear her chiding her. "Sarah, what in the world are you doing? He's way too young for you."

"I like him, Megs. He's everything I need right now."

Both girls looked over at Billy. Megan scowled while Sarah smiled and fiddled with a strand of her blond hair, twirling it around a finger.

"You didn't... you know?"

"We might have kissed a little," Sarah said, putting Megan's greater concerns at ease.

Megan gasped. "Oh, my god, Sarah. You're so bad. He's like... fourteen."

"Fifteen. And I'm sixteen going on seventeen."

"You're seventeen in a week. He's barely sprouted any chest hair, yet."

"Look," Sarah said, glancing over at us and then at Megan. "I like him. So, sue me."

Megan stared long and hard at Sarah and then her big bright smile ignited like a million suns and she grabbed Sarah and drew her into her bosom, squeezing her so tightly that her face when blue from lack of oxygen.

"Can't… breathe… " Sarah wheezed, trying to squirm out of Megan's bear-hug but failing miserably.

Megan finally let go and Sarah braced her hands on her needs and gasped for air. Megan then stomped up to Billy and, towering over him, she looked down at him and placed a finger on his chest. "You look after my girl, you here?"

"I will," Billy said.

"If you hurt her, I'll crush your balls in my fist until they ooze between my fingers like raspberry jelly. Got that?"

"Harsh," Mitch gulped. Paul stood next to him nodding silently.

"Overly graphic," Paul added.

"I hear you," Billy answered, "and—"

Before he could finish his sentence, Megan ball-tapped him and dropped him to his knees. Then, spinning about, she tossed her hair, which whipped him in his face, stepped off the lawn onto the driveway and skated back into the garage.

We all gathered inside the house and Melody set a large dinner plate with a stack of ham and cheese sandwiches onto the kitchen table.

"Mom and I made these for everyone before

everything happened. She said you should all eat, keep your strength up."

"Thank you," Paul said, grabbing two sandwiches and taking two big bites. Talking with his mouth open, he added, "I'm starving."

Billy, Mitch, and I helped ourselves to one each and I passed the plate around to the girls. Sarah took one, Megan took two, and Melody took three although I knew she wouldn't be able to finish it all.

"You got any chips, Billy?" Paul asked, flecks of food spilling out of his mouth.

Billy nodded, went over to the cupboard, and fetched a bag of classic Lay's potato chips. He pulled open the bag and dumped them into a big mixing bowl for everyone to share.

We ate our food in silence, all but for the crunching of chips. When we'd finished, Billy said, "Let's gear up and get to the drugstore. It's already noon and I for one want to get back home before dark."

Everyone nodded and we gathered our stuff. Billy packed his crossbow, Sarah had given Melody Jimmy "Mad Dog" Polson's knife. Meanwhile, Megan grabbed her hockey stick and strapped a machete to her back. Mitch grabbed the baseball bat that he'd pounded nails into, making it a spiked bat, and, last but not least, I picked up the Samurai sword that Billy's dad had brought back from Vietnam. Granted, it wasn't a genuine sword, since Samurai were Japanese. But it was a good replica.

Paul walked over to the garage wall and pulled down the pump-action shotgun and grabbed a box of slugs. "What are you doing?" asked Billy, questioning Paul grabbing a gun when nobody had completed their gun-training yet.

Paul stuffed the ammunition in his backpack and then fished around until he drew out a paperback novel. Tossing the book to Billy, he caught it and looked down at the title; *Lord of the Flies.*

"Are you trying to tell me you've had that in your bag all along?" asked Mitch. "We're supposed to read that before Drake will allow us to use any of the guns."

"I already passed my test," Paul said. "And I read it last summer," he added, resting the shotgun across his shoulders and pushing up his classes.

"You're joking," Mitch replied, a twinge of jealousy in his voice.

"No, he's not," I answered. "I was there. I saw

Drake say that Paul was ready."

"My, man," Billy said, holding out a fist for an obligatory fist bump. Instead, Paul, being the nerd he was, didn't know what to do with it and placed his hand on Billy's fist and gave it a small jiggle and then broke away. Billy shrugged and, without wasting any further time, walked over and handed Sarah his crossbow.

"Wait, what will you use?" she asked, looking down at the crossbow she held in her hands.

Billy smiled and said, "I'm glad you asked." He walked over to an old trunk in the back of the garage, opened it, and drew out a Homelite XL chainsaw. Starting it up, it rumbled and buzzed, and he shouted above the whirring blade, "I'm going to use this!"

"That settles it," Melody said, as Billy cut the power and stopped the chainsaw. "We're a team of royal mother-flippin' badasses."

"Language!" I said.

"What?!" said Melody, defensively. "Badass isn't a bad word. Besides, I say worse stuff all the time."

I laughed. "I'm not the one you need to convince. It's Mom you've gotta take that argument up with," I replied.

Sarah stepped in and, crouching down, looked Melody directly in her eyes. "Besides, using foul language is not very lady like."

Melody let out a defeated sigh and replied, "I guess you're right."

With the drama of the day resolved, which seemed trivial compared to the reality of having to deal with a genuine alien invasion, we hit the road. Ten minutes later we were walking down the center of the street that ran through the center of town.

"It's like a ghost-town," Paul said, glancing to his left and then right.

He wasn't' wrong either. The entire town seemed deserted. Nothing so much as stirred. All the people had either gone home or were in hiding. That's when Billy threw up a fist and said, "Everyone, quiet. Paul, on me."

Paul drew up next to Billy, shotgun in hand. "What is it," whispered Paul.

We all fell in line, single-file, behind Billy and Paul while Mitch and Melody watched our six.

"What's the four-one-one," Megan asked, tapping he hockey stick on the ground.

Billy pointed. "Over there. That military jeep

parked in front of the Ace Hardware. Something is off about it."

"What do you mean?" asked Sarah, squinting over at the jeep.

"The front side panel is all dented in, like it tried to ram something."

"Or something rammed into it," Mitch added. He looked side to side, scanning our surroundings to make sure there weren't any more of those things lingering in the shadows of alleyways or nearby groves of trees.

Billy looked over he shoulder at us and said, "Stay here. I'm going to check it out."

"Not without me," Sarah said, jogging up to join him.

We all held back as they drew closer to the vehicle, taking it slow and easy. They arrived at the jeep and Billy touched the hood and whispered, "It's still warm."

Sarah heard a noise and raised the crossbow and pointed it at the side of the building that led into the alley.

"What was that?" she asked.

"What was what?" Billy asked, gripping the

chainsaw tightly.

"You didn't hear that?"

He held out the chainsaw in front of himself as he walked toward the alley. Sarah followed him, aiming a freshly racked bolt just over his shoulder.

They rounded the corner and I about lost sight of them when they came sprinting back around. "Go, go, go!" shouted Billy. He waved his hand at us motioning for us to flee when a massive alien bounded off the side of the building, leaped into the air, and pounced onto the jeep, crushing it in as if it were made of tinfoil.

Billy let Sarah run on ahead and he turned around and gave the chainsaw a few cranks. But it wouldn't start up. So, spinning around like a shotput thrower, he lobbed the chainsaw into the air, throwing it at the alien. The chainsaw missed and crashed down next to the monster.

This got the beast's attention, and the it squawked and growled at the contraption, and then bit it, shook it around like a dog does a chew toy, and then let go of it. The bent and deformed chainsaw fell to the ground with a clank and the beast's attention returned to us.

That's when I noticed the alien's side was scorched with what appeared to be shotgun blasts. Was this the same creature from earlier that Billy's mom had chased away? If so, I'm guessing it remembered us. Because it wasn't all too happy.

"Oh, Cheez-It crackers!" Mitch yelled, as he turned and ran. Megan shoved Paul, to get him moving and then followed him. Billy and Sarah were fast upon me and I joined them.

We'd made it about two hundred meters when I realized that Melody was nowhere to be seen. I looked back to find her standing her ground, not moving an inch, fists balled up as the alien, the size of a large African rhinoceros, stood in front of her, snorting and pawing at the ground angrily.

The creature blinked its six eyes and opened its fanged jowls and let out a ferocious roar.

Melody's hair fluttered about in the current of its rancid breath, but other than making a sour face from the bad-smelling breath, she didn't budge. "You don't scare me," Melody said, balling her fists up even tighter.

"Melody!" I yelled as I craned my neck to see her. Mid-stride, I planted my feet, skidded to a halt—nearly falling on my face. Luckily, I caught myself with one arm, pushed myself back up, and turned back toward Melody.

As I ran back toward her, I realized that she was too far to get to in time. The alien monster had already reared up on its hind quarters and raised its massive claws to strike her down.

*"Noooo!"* I shouted, stretching out my hand and fingers toward her—wishing against all hope that I could somehow reach her in time and snatch her back from harm's way. But it simply wasn't possible.

In my state of panic, everything seemed to slow down. My surroundings moved lethargically around me as my mind went into hyper-drive and I strained against gravity to move even just one step closer to my sister.

But for every step I took the creatures arm fell several inches. Meaning, by the time I reached Melody there'd be nothing left but a bloody stump.

A bolt whizzed by my ear and I watched as it nailed the creature's bicep, just above the elbow. It roared, and stepped back, circled in an agitated manner and then hissed at us all.

Melody took a step back and I looked back to see

Sarah loading a second bolt. When I turned back I saw the creature ram into Melody with his head.

It struck her in the chest and sent her flying backward about ten feet. She hit the asphalt with a thud and was trying to push herself up when the creature landed directly in front of her. It placed both front paws on either side of my sister, straddling her, and then roared in her face.

She began crying and I turned back toward Paul. Our eyes met and he knew exactly what I was going to ask. Paul tossed the shotgun to me and I caught it mid-air, and, in one fluid motion, spun around, and aimed the menacing barrel right at the creature's head.

"Get away from my sister, you ugly piece of—"

"GRAAAAAHHHK!" the creature squawked. It sounded like how I'd imagine a tyrannosaurus rex might sound. Halfway between a squawk and a roar. It then shook its head and unfurled its six barbed tails.

I cocked the shotgun and, not wanting to accidentally hit Melody, I shot a warning shot into the air. This only made the monster angrier, and it clawed the pavement, leaving three massive gouges in the asphalt next to Melody's head.

"Shoot it!" Billy shouted.

"I might hit my sister," I shouted back.

This was what was called a Catch-22. No matter what you chose, paradoxically, all choices led to the same undesirable result. Either, I accidentally shoot my sister, and she's dead. Or, if I don't shoot, the monster mauls her to death, and we're back to my sister being dead again.

Gritting my teeth, I aimed the gun and took deep breaths. *Here goes nothing,* I thought. Without a moment to spare, I slowly squeezed down on the trigger, but before I could fire off a shot, a black blur came charging through the grove of trees from across the street. Whatever it was, it was fast, and sprinted straight for the alien and my sister—not slowing until it rammed the side of the alien at top speed.

Both creatures tumbled to the ground and rolled about in a cat-like skirmish. Eventually, they both sprung up and began hissing at one another.

"What the…" I began to say, but I was lacking the words for what I was seeing.

What we all witnessed in that moment defied description. The alien from two nights ago, the one which had stalked us in the woods, and followed us to Fort Liberty for an inevitable standoff had come out of nowhere and smashed into the larger alien.

The large alien staggered back and hissed at the smaller alien. Then, the smaller one whipped its purple glowing tails and sliced the bigger one across its face.

Confused by the attack by its own brethren, the big alien squawked again and making a prompt retreat, turned and lumbered off.

We all watched in dumfounded amazement as Melody rose up to her feat, pulled a Kit-kat out of her pocket, peeled the wrapper away and held the chocolate bar out for the smaller alien to take.

It slowly inched up to her, almost timid, and with the very tip of its teeth, delicately snatched the chocolate out of her hands.

Melody giggled and reached out and patted the alien on its head as it snarfed down the Kit-kat. It's six eyes closed and it seemed to make a purring sound as she petted it. Was it showing my little sister affection?

"It likes chocolate," Melody announced, turning toward us and smiling the brightest, most fearless smile any of us had ever seen.

# 4

## INVASION
### PART 4: COMPLETE THE MISSION

NONE OF US KNEW WHAT TO SAY. WE STOOD
thunderstruck, watching in silence as my little sister
patted the head of a lethal killing machine—the same
creature that chased us through the woods that fateful
night, that laid siege on us at Fort Liberty, and that
tried to maul us all to death as little as a couple of days
ago.

"Are you guys seeing this?" Paul asked.

We all nodded. Even though we couldn't believe
our eyes, it was all really happening. My sister had,
against all odds, made friends with the alien.

"He's actually quite friendly," Melody said, patting
the monster's head some more. He also can do tricks.
Watch!"

She pulled out a second Kit-kat from her pocket,

unwrapped it, and then cocked her arm back as though she was going to throw it.

"Fetch, boy! Fetch!"

The alien spun in energetic circles then hopped back, its butt wiggling like that of an excited dog. Melody launched the chocolate through the air and the creature took off after it.

Leaping into the air, the alien caught the chocolate, landed, and ate it. Licking its lips, it trotted up to Melody, it's long tongue lapping at its own face, making sure to get every last bit of chocolate.

Melody laughed and said, "Good boy!" She patted the alien's head again and it sat down beside her. It panted as it sat and stared at us. Although it didn't seem to be a threat in the moment, we were all still a little bit hesitant. After all, it had killed all of Sarah's friends at Make-out Point that terrible night.

"Do you think it remembers us?" Mitch whispered.

"Yeah, I'm pretty sure," I answered. "The other one remembered us and it only met us in a fleeting moment of turmoil. We had a full on brawl and nearly burned down the forest fighting this thing."

"In that case," Mitch gulped, "we're dead meat."

"What are you all so scared about?" Megan asked. "It seems harmless." She walked up to Melody and the creature and the creature skidded back, nervous about this new human.

"It's all right," Melody said, reaching out a hand. "She's a friend."

The creature cautiously approached Megan and sniffed her hand. Then his began to sniff her pockets and other crevasses in search of chocolate. When it got near her crotch she hopped back and said, "Whoa there, big guy. You won't find chocolate there."

"Check the other end!" Mitch shouted. "There might be some in there." He laughed at his own joke.

Megan turned around and flipped her brother the bird. Before she could say anything, however, the creature nudged her from behind with its head. She laughed and turned around to pat its head. "Who's a good boy?" she asked, speaking in the cutesy baby-talk that pet owners always used with their animals. "You are! You're a good boy!"

"See," Melody said. "He likes you."

"Although I hate to admit it, he saved our lives," Sarah added, bringing our attention to the fact that if it hadn't intervened, we may have all been dead within moments.

"What now?" Paul pushed his glasses up and looked at me and Billy.

I looked at Billy, waiting for him to make the final call. He scanned all our faces and said, "We carry on with the mission. Just, you know, with an alien in tow."

"You sure you can keep in under control?" I asked Melody. She nodded.

"As long as we have chocolate, it'll behave."

"That settles it, then," said Billy. "We have ourselves a pet alien."

"Just one question," I asked. "What should we call it."

"I named him Lucy," Melody replied.

"Lucy?" Paul asked, a puzzled look on his face. "How do you figure?"

"Because I like the name Lucy. And he looks like a Lucy."

"You know Lucy is a female name, right?" asked Megan.

"Duh," Melody replied sarcastically.

"Lucy it is, then," Billy said. He cleared his throat and looked up at the sky. Holding his hand up the shield his eyes from the sun, he added, "We'd best get a move on. Time is a wasting and we're burning daylight."

We all began our gradual march up the street, determined to make it to the drugstore. Half a block later, I paused and looked back to see Sarah standing in place, still not moving. Tears were streaming down her face and her hands were trembling.

Megan noticed it at the same time I had and ran over to her and got to her just as Sarah collapsed to her knees. Catching her in her arms, Megan said, "Don't worry, I've got you."

Noticing that something was up, Billy turned and began to head toward the girls when I raised my hand and gestured for him to hold off. "I think she just needs time to process it all. It's a lot to take in. Especially knowing that that thing killed all of her friends."

"Oh, dang," Mitch said. "That's right. It slaughtered everyone at Make-out Point."

We all looked back toward Melody and her new pet, which was the size of a large bear. They walked side-by-side up the street, not a care in the world.

"I don't know if these things are intelligent like us, but if it can be trained…," I said, thinking out loud,

"If it can be conditioned to like humans, then we need to find a way to use that to our advantage."

Megan helped Sarah up and I turned to her and looked her straight in her ocean blue eyes. Sarah had been Melody and my baby sister since we were little. She'd known my family for the past five years and, honestly, she was like an older sister to me. "Are you going to be all right?"

"Yeah, I think so." She sniffled and then wiped her nose with the back of her hand. Billy strode up and handed her a handkerchief. She took it and dapped her eyes dry with it.

"Keep it," he said.

She smiled at him. "Thanks."

"Come on, you slow pokes!" Melody shouted.

I turned and smiled at her. Then, I looked back at the rest of the gang, and with a wave of my hand, I gestured for them to go on ahead of me.

"Shall we?"

Billy Bardem was the first to step up and resume the mission. Get to the drugstore. Find medicine and supplies. Then, slowly, we all turned and followed him up the street together.

Sure, we knew the risks. Other alien monsters

were most certainly roaming about the town. The military could drop a bomb on our heads at any moment. But for some reason, we found that we no longer feared the unknown.

When we arrived at the Walgreens, the windows were busted out and glass scattered the ground. A group of people jumped out the windows, arms full of beer.

"Melody," Sarah said, motioning for my sister to hold up. Sarah obviously didn't want to get to close to the creatures, seeing she still had reservations about it.

"What's up?"

"When we get inside the store, you stay close to me and Megan. While the boys find the medicine that's on your mom's list, we'll get supplies."

"Including feminine products," added Megan.

"Ew," Mitch said. "Too much information, sis."

"Tampons, Maxi-pads, and Ibuprofen for menstrual cramps," Megan informed, saying it loudly so that it would bother her brother even more. "Those sorts of things."

Mitch pretended to gag and Paul sniggered but really it wasn't all that funny. Only young boys who didn't know the difference between a girl and a woman got weirded out by that sort of thing. And only guys who never wanted to be with a girlfriend would be stupid enough to joke about it.

"Oh, grow up, dick-weed," Melody said. "You act like that around a real woman and you're destined to die a virgin."

"Yeah, dick-weed," Megan said, nodding in agreement with Melody. She looked down at my sis and winked at her, letting her know that she had her back.

When it came to girls, Mitch wasn't the most experienced. He'd probably be the last of us to have a girlfriend, and that's assuming he grew out of his awkward nerdy-Dungeon's-and-Dragons-phase. Not that girls didn't play D&D. Many did, but none of them wanted anything to do with him.

Paul slapped Mitch on his back so hard it was sure to leave a welt. "Melody might be right about you dying a virgin."

"You're one to talk," Mitch said, scowling at his friend. "You don't have a girlfriend either."

"Yeah, but I'm not trying to get a girlfriend. All you've done is say, ooh, Sarah this, and, ahh, Sarah that." Paul rested his chin on his interlocked finger-bridge and batted his eyes.

Mitch grew flush with embarrassment, looked over at Sarah and then Paul and then stormed off. As he walked to the back of the store he slapped some items of an endcap display out of frustration and then disappeared around a corner.

Paul instantly regretted making fun of his friend. It was a little bit mean to insist he wouldn't ever find a girl, as if he wasn't lovable. Paul looked at everyone who were silent observers. "Maybe I should go talk to him?"

"No, I'll do it," Sarah said, putting down an arm full of things she'd gathered. "It's better if it comes from me."

I kept my eye on Sarah until she disappeared around the isle full of baby stuff, including formula and diapers. Mitch was somewhere behind the isle pouting. And, although I couldn't see her, I could hear her just fine.

"What's the matter, bud?"

"The guys know I have a crush on you. I've had a crush on you since the third grade. And they know I'll never get anyone as smart or pretty as you."

"That's not true," Sarah said.

"It's not?" Mitch asked.

"Well, you're a smart young man. You have interests beyond just girls. High school girls are fickle. They'll go for the good looking guys every time. But wait until you get into college. You'll be getting good grades, you'll be in clubs, and the girls will start to notice that you're more interesting than the slew of brainless jocks they dated in high school."

"Do you really think so?"

"I do."

"Can I hug you?" asked Mitch. "I just didn't want you thinking I was trying to cop a feel."

"Yes," Sarah laughed. "You may hug me."

There was a long silence and we all heard Mitch whisper, "Marry me."

"What was that?" asked Sarah, feigning ignorance.

"Nothing," Mitch said, clearing his throat. "It was nothing."

"Riiight," Sarah replied skeptically.

After about a minute of silence, Sarah and Mitch finally came out from around the corner of the aisle and looked at everyone who suddenly started to pretend to be busier than they actually were.

"GRAAAAAHHHK!"

"Holy sardines!" Paul gasped, clutching his chest. "I forgot that thing was still with us."

"What is it, Lucy? Did you hear something?" Melody walked up to Lucy who sat in front of the main entrance staring out the sliding doors, which were fractured and missing a pane of glass, when suddenly the roar of a stampede could be heard.

"Do you guys hear that?" I asked. I approached the front door, careful not to step on the alien's six tails that just gently swayed back and forth like that of a shark's tail cutting through the shallows.

I held my finger up to my mouth and hushed everyone as I peeked out of the broken windows. An entire stampede of alien beasts, like Lucy, were charging up main street and I quickly spun around and waved at everyone to hide behind the shelves and countertops. I raced back and slid, as if I were sliding into first on a baseball diamond, and Billy grabbed me and reeled me into him just as the first few aliens rushed by.

We waited for probably sixty seconds but it felt like an eternity. We all tried our best to breathe shallow, keeping our sounds minimal. That's when there was a loud crash and I slowly turned my head to peer between the shelves on the rack. One of the aliens had burst through the entrance and was sniffing the air, looking for what I could only assume was us—looking for its next kill.

Melody held Lucy back, but Lucy shook free and then trotted out of the aisle and into the store by the cash registers. The other alien perked its head up and its tails whipped about frantically, like an angry twitchy cat tail and looked directly at Lucy.

Lucy merely raised a leg and peed on the counter with the register then looked at its alien brethren, and then sat down and began panting heavily.

The other alien snorted, squawked lightly, then turned and ran back out to join the hunting party.

"Good boy, Lucy," Megan said.

Lucy looked at all of us with big innocent eyes, like those of a puppy, and panted some more. We all looked at one another and I could tell we were all thinking the same thing—whether or not it was safe to go outside.

"What's the plan, Billy?" Mitch asked.

We all turned to Billy. Although he hadn't volunteered to be the leader of our group, he was our de facto leader by popular vote. Billy thought for a moment then looked at Sarah. She seemed to know what he was thinking because she nodded, as if to say, it's going to be all right.

Billy cleared his throat and then looked at all of us. "I hate to say this, but we stand a better chance of making it back alive if we split up into separate groups."

"That makes sense," Paul said, nodding.

"The only question is, who goes with who," I said.

We all stood up and moved to the area in front of the pharmacy where we had gathered all our supplies.

"Paul, Mitch, Sarah and I will branch off as one group. You," Billy said, looking at me, "your sister, and Megan will be in the other group."

"Lucy will come with us," Melody added.

We all shook hands and hugged and gathered are supplies and then, Billy's team snuck out the back exit and my team, along with Lucy, went out the front.

As night settled over Woodridge, blanketing our town with a velvet sky full of stars, we kept to the shadows of the side streets and avoided any unnecessary contact.

In the distance, all the way on the other side of

town by the power company, there was a loud explosion, lots of sparks, and orange and blue flames.

Military gunfire lit up the night in bursts of flashes and bangs. The two Warthog fighter jets streaked overhead and dropped a couple of bombs. The blast shook the entire town and the gunfire momentarily ceased then started up again.

"I hope Billy and the others are okay," Melody said.

I nodded. "Me too."

Megan looked back at the creature. "Um, I know this thing is a killing machine, but so far it's been nothing but helpful."

We all looked over at Lucy who promptly sat in the street and lifted a leg, tucked its head under, and began licking itself.

"Uh, yeah," I said. "A real joy to be around."

"You know what I meant," Megan laughed, hitting me in the arm.

I laughed again, feeling a real connection with her, and when our eyes locked, there was a long intense moment between us. At least, it felt that way to me.

Unexpected as it all was, I realized I could fall in

love with her in an instant. She must have felt something too, because she quickly looked away and began twirling a lock of her golden hair around her finger.

"We should, uh, probably keep moving."

"Agreed," Melody said. She then whipped out a Kit-kat and waved it in the air. "Lucy! Come here, boy!"

Lucy trotted up to Melody and gently took the candy from her little twelve year old hand. As if feeding an alien chocolate was perfectly normal, Melody spun on her heels and began to cheerfully skip up the road. Lucy followed after her like a young duckling following its mother.

"She really has that thing trained," Megan said.

"I'm still hesitant to let her keep it," I said, unable to hide my trepidation. "After all, it did kill a whole bunch of kids."

"I know," Megan replied in a solemn tone. "Most of them were my friends. My classmates."

"I'm sorry," I said. "I couldn't imagine losing my friends all in one night. It's horrific, to say the least."

"I appreciate the sympathy," she replied. "But we don't know anything about these creatures, and it might have been just as scared as everyone else. When a porcupine pricks you with its quills, it's not because it's out to get you. It's scared and is trying its best to survive. I think maybe that's Lucy in a nutshell."

"That's a fair assessment," I said, agreeing with her sentiment. "If Lucy's homeworld was destroyed and all the aliens like him have been floating through space for decades, maybe hibernating along the way, then, yeah, I'd be pretty startled ending up on an alien world not my own, too."

"You know, Travis, you're actually pretty smart, for a fourteen year old."

"And you're actually pretty, uh, hot for an older sister. I mean, not my sister. That'd be gross. But, you know, Mitch's sister. It's, like, hard to believe you both came out of the same parents."

Megan laughed. "Were you trying to pay me a compliment just now?"

"Yeah," I said, kicking myself for my bumbling and nonsensical speech. "It sort of came out weird."

"So, you think I'm hot?"

I nodded. "Yeah. I mean, have you seen yourself? Who wouldn't?"

Megan smiled at me again. This time, though,

tears glistened in her eyes and she wiped the corner of her eye with her thumb, and laughed at herself.

"What's wrong?" I asked.

"It's nothing. It's stupid. But hearing you call me pretty just now triggered something. I guess, with Mitch always calling me ugly, fat, and making fun of my looks, I've just never had any confidence in myself. And then, here you are, and you think I'm pretty and I turning into a blubbering idiot."

"You're not an idiot," I said. I reached out and touched Megan's arm. She looked down at my hand and then my eyes. We shared another moment and she laughed again.

"Yeah, well, that doesn't mean I don't always feel like one."

"You need to stop being so hard on yourself. I've been to your house dozens of times to hang out with Mitch. And every time I'd visit I'd peek into your bedroom as I walked by just to see if you were there. I was always happy when you'd look up from your phone call while talking to friends just to shoot me a friendly smile. You always made me feel welcome."

"Wow," Megan replied, wiping the last tear away. "I guess I didn't realize you liked spying on me in my bedroom.”

“What?” I balked, shocked by her insinuation. “I’d never… I mean, it was completely innocent, I swear!”

Megan laughed and grabbed my shoulders. “Relax, Travis. I’m just teasing you.”

“Oh,” I said, taking a deep breath.

Her hands resting on my shoulders, she stared at me, our eyes connecting on some deeper level. Before the long pause grew too awkward, however, Megan gently shoved me back and spun around.

“It’s okay if you think I’m hot, Trav. You’re pretty cute yourself.”

My words failed me and all I could do was stand in shock as I watched her head back up the hill to rejoin my sister and Lucy, who were waiting patiently half a block up the street.

Smitten didn’t even begin to describe how I felt about Megan. I mean, Megan McIntyre, one of the hottest high school girls in all of Woodridge, had called me cute just now. It took me a minute to regain my composure, but I finally found my voice again and called out, “Hey, wait for me,” as I jogged up the street to catch up to the girls.

With Lucy by our side, we walked back to Billy

Bardem's house. Or, rather, what was left of it.

Once we arrived back at Billy's house, we could scarcely believe what we found—which to be precise, was a whole lot of nothing. Devastatingly, Billy's entire house was gone. Completely obliterated by a bomb. Probably one of the bombs we saw being dropped earlier, when we were leaving the drugstore.

All that remained now, sadly, was a giant crater with some leaky pipes jutting out, a pool of water gradually filling the bottom of the crater.

"Well, that sucks," I said, placing my hands on my hips. Melody leaned over the edge and looked down into the crater.

"Trav," Melody asked.

"Yeah?"

"What do we do now?"

"We do as we agreed to do. Meet up at Fort Liberty."

"And," Megan added, "if we get there first, we wait for the others."

Satisfied with that answer, Melody nodded and then headed in the direction of the woods, Lucy trailing behind her.

I held out my hand for Megan to take and she

looked down at it. She stared for the longest time, as if she were a little reluctant, not knowing what kind of mixed-signals it would be sending me if she chose to take it. But then, to my pleasant surprise, she reached out and took my hand in hers.

Before I could react, she reeled me in and gave me the biggest hug of my life. "Thank you, Travis. For being such a great kid."

"Jeez, you two. Get a room," Melody said, pausing long enough to look back and give us grief.

"That thought, young lady," Megan said, "hadn't even crossed my mind." Then Megan paused and looked at me one more time, stroked her chin contemplatively, and then added, "Well, maybe in a few years."

My cheeks flushed with embarrassment and I turned my face away, unable to restrain the giant smile that had spread from ear to ear.

"Until then, you'll need to be patient and wait." Megan leaned down and gave me a peck on the cheek and followed it up with a firm slap, shocking me back to reality.

"Uh, thanks?" I said, rubbing the sting out of my cheek. "I think."

I looked back over my shoulder and scanned the darkened town for signs of movement. But there was nothing. Billy and the others were on their own. At least, for tonight.

# 5

## INVASION
### PART 5: DEFENDERS OF WOODRIDGE

It was odd to think we were back at Fort Liberty, where it had all begun. While Melody, Megan, and I slept up in the treehouse, Lucy slept down on the ground by the foot of the tree trunk.

Melody snored lightly, as she slept between Megan and me. When I rolled over, I saw Megan's wide-open baby-blue eyes staring at me in the moonlight.

"What's the matter?" I asked.

There was a long pause, she smiled briefly, and then replied, "I've been thinking and I've gotta ask you something. Why don't you have a girlfriend, Travis?"

"I don't know. I guess I just wasn't interested in girls till recently."

"Do you want one?"

"You mean like, you?"

She laughed quietly, glancing down at Melody to make sure she didn't disturb her. "In your dreams, Don Juan." She smiled again, to let me know she was just teasing. After a long pause, she asked. "Have you ever kissed a girl?"

I shook my head. "No," I replied. Rolling onto my back, I looked up at the stars through the slats of the treehouse roof. They sparkled from millions of light years away but, somehow, gave me a sense of calm.

"Why not?"

"The chance really hasn't presented itself, I suppose."

"Do you want to kiss me?" Megan asked.

"Oh, I don't know," I answered, still gazing up at the sky that shone through the crevices in the ceiling.

"What do you mean you don't know?" she asked in a less than amused, almost wounded tone.

"I mean, what with my sister here, laying between us, sharing a kiss right now would seem a little bit weird. Wouldn't it? Of course I want to, don't get me wrong. It's just that… I don't know how," I confessed.

When there hadn't been any reply, or response to my admission of inexperience at all for that matter, I turned to find Megan fast asleep. "Megan? Megan," I whispered, trying to get her attention, but it was no use. She was out like a light.

I let out a pent up sigh and then reached over and pulled her blanket over her shoulders so she'd stay warm. I then rolled onto my side, facing away from my sister and Megan, and slowly fell asleep.

The night was peaceful, more or less. The only difficult thing was how ridiculously cold it had gotten during the night. When dawn's golden rays broke over the horizon, I slowly sat up, rubbed the sleep out of my eyes, and looked over to find Melody curled up inside Megans arms. Megan was clutching onto my sister as though she were a Teddy bear.

Unfortunately, there was no sign of Billy or the others. I slowly rose to my feet, reached around my own torso with my hands and rubbed my arms for warmth.

Stepping onto the balcony, I looked down to find that Lucy had crept over to the foliage and was nestled up under a thick grove of spruce trees. Probably to get out of the sunlight, which irritated its sensitive skin.

Returning to the treehouse, I watched as Megan sat straight up and, pressing a hand between her legs as she pinched her thighs together, trying her best not to squirm, she said, "I've really got to pee."

Melody, still half asleep, raised her arm and pointed a little finger at the back corner where the camping toilet was. "Bucket," she said in a dreary voice.

Her little arm collapsed back into bed and I looked up as Megan raced to the bucket, pulled down her pants with haste, and squatted over the bucket. She had to go so badly that she hadn't even waited for me to divert my eyes, which I did anyway.

"I'll give you some privacy," I said, turning toward the door.

"Wait, Travis," she said. I paused without looking back. "Can you hand me some toilet paper?"

"Oh, uh, yeah. No problem," I replied. I grabbed the extra roll from inside the bench hutch and then walked backward to hand it to her.

"Over here," she said. "Nope. More to the left. No, not your left, my left."

"Right," I said, correcting my mistake.

She took the tissue paper from me and being super grateful for my help, sighed a heartfelt, "Thanks."

My back to her, I answered, "No problem. Anytime."

I left her to finish her business and stepped out of the treehouse. Once outside, I took in a refreshing breath of morning air and then slowly let it out.

Another few minutes passed and Megan joined me out on the deck. She didn't say anything but merely leaned on the railing next to me and then, leaning over, nudged me with her shoulder and smiled.

"I'm sorry if I weirded you out," she said. "But I'm really glad you're here with me."

"It beats getting stuck with Mitch, I suppose," I said. This caused Megan to let out a blast of laughter so loud she surprised even herself and quickly covered her mouth with both hands to muffle her unexpected outburst.

"Could you imagine him handing me toilet paper as I sat on the porcelain throne?"

"No," I said. "I'm fairly certain he would have left you on that toilet for the rest of all time," I replied.

"Yeah," Megan agreed, "I think you're probably right."

We stood, our shoulders touching, and watched the sunrise grow from pink to orange and then slowly grow diluted as a great blue sky took its place.

"Last night you said you wanted to kiss me, then fell asleep." I looked over at her and she met my gaze then turned away. Her face remained serious and we lingered in silence for another minute or so.

"Let me promise you this much… If we make it through this week alive, I will give you that kiss. Until then, just realize that I'm kinda nuts."

"I wouldn't have you any other way," I replied, and nudged her back with my shoulder.

She laughed and we both looked out across the trees that trailed down the hill toward the crater where Billy Bardem's house used to be.

That's when we saw them.

"Hey, guys!" I shouted, jumping up and waving my hands. "Over here!"

Sure enough, Sarah, Billy, Mitch and Paul had survived the night and were trekking up the trailhead as they made their way to Fort Liberty.

Lucy raised his head, looked around, but deeming it not a threat, tucked his head back under his large taloned leg and went back to sleep.

"Hmmph. So much for our guard dog," Megan said with a huff.

We left Melody sleeping peacefully in a pile of cozy blankets and climbed down the rope latter, meeting the group at the base of the treehouse. As they came into camp, we saw their miserable faces.

"What happened to you guys?" I asked.

"It's a long story," Billy replied. "But we haven't slept a wink and we've been walking all night." He dropped the basket of supplies they'd been carrying onto the ground and a palpable wave of relief washed over him.

"In that case, you all head on up to get some sleep while Travis and I head back into town and try to scavenge up some breakfast. Maybe we can find some eggs and a frying pan or two to make a simple breakfast for everyone."

Mitch yawned which triggered Paul to yawn too and then Sarah. Sarah reached over and touched Megan's arm. "Stay safe. There's more of those things out there than we thought. And they're hunting us."

"Yeah," Paul said. "It took us half the night to ditch them. They seem to have heat vision and can find you even when you're hiding behind a wall. Which is why they hunt at night as opposed to the day."

Mitch was already on his way to the top of the stairs when Billy covered his mouth and masked his own yawn.

"See y'all later," Billy said. He waved to us without looking back and continued up the stairs.

"Yeah," Paul said, as he followed both Mitch and Billy. Letting out another big yawn, he added in a dreary voice, "See you guys in a few winks."

Sarah held back and looked over at Megan, then looked at me, and, then Megan again. She raised a suspicious eyebrow, somehow sensing something was going on between us.

"What?" asked Megan.

"Nothing," Sarah said, smiling deviously.

"I don't like the way you're smiling right now," Megan said.

"How am I smiling?" asked Sarah, her smile growing even bigger.

"Like that," Megan said waving a finger in Sarah's face. "Exactly like that."

"I have a sixth sense about these things."

"You're imagining things because you're sleep deprived."

"You like him!" Sarah said, teasing Megan. "You,

like, *LIKE* like him!"

"Don't be ridiculous. He's my kid brother's friend. You need to get some sleep, young lady," Megan said escorting Sarah to the staircase.

Sarah looked back over her shoulder. "You be careful, Travis. This one's a man eater!"

"Oh, you hush!" Megan chastised with a playful laugh. Megan grabbed both of Sarah's butt cheeks and pushed her up the stairs.

"Yeesh, girl. I'm going. I'm going!"

"Not... fast... enough," Megan said through gritted teeth.

Finally Sarah laughed and then headed up the stairs of her own volition. Megan, standing halfway up the stairs turned, threw one hand on her hip, and looked at me.

"What's a man-eater?" I asked.

Megan's cheeks flushed bright pink and she waved her hand. "Oh, that? It's nothing. Just ignore her."

I chuckled and then motioned for her to follow me. "Come on, Megs. We've got a lot of ground to cover in just a few hours. And since the town is overrun, we'll stick to the residential areas and see if anyone else has survived or, you know, packed up and got the heck out of Dodge."

"That's rather dire," Megan said, drawing up next to me. "I just hope those creatures haven't killed more people."

"I hope those creatures don't kill us," I added.

She nodded wholeheartedly with that sentiment. "You and me both, kid. You and me both."

We walked side by side over to the log bench that Billy's brother, Marvin, had carved a couple of summers back and picked up our weapons. After we strapped our weapons to our backs, the samurai sword for me and the hockey stick for her, I looked up to find her staring at me. She stared at me with such intensity that it caused me to gulp down butterflies.

"What is it, Megs?"

"I liked it when you called me Megs, just now."

"Oh," I said, not knowing what she meant by that. After all, it was her name. "I'm glad for you."

Megan laughed louder than she needed to and then playfully smacked my arm. "You're so hilarious," she said.

Even though the way she had said it was oddly manic, I just rolled with it. "I am?"

"Yeah, silly. You're not annoying like my dick-weed brother." We started walking again and Megan continued lamenting on the hardships of big-sisterhood. "I mean, he farts in his sleep. He farts when he's awake. If he could, he'd probably fart while he's farting. He has no concept of personal boundaries."

"How do you mean?" I asked, my curiosity genuinely piqued.

"Well, I bet you never walk in on your sister when she's using the bathroom."

"Heck, no," I answered. "My mom would kill me."

"See, that's how it should be. But my family only has the one bathroom and we have to share. And I'll be in the middle of taking a shower and he'll burst in and take a dump and stink up the whole bathroom."

"Yeah, I can see how that would suck," I said, sympathizing with Megan. If she knew the truth, that Mitch did that just to bother her, she'd probably lose it and strangle the kid to death.

"He also took a recording of all his little friends talking about me..." Megan paused, and I looked up at her face to see genuine tears. She sniffled and wiped the tears away. "He left a tape in my Walkman that recorded a conversation y'all had here at Fort Liberty about how you all wanted to see me naked and how you wanted to fling mud at me."

"Oh," I said, feeling humbled by the fact that our juvenile ribbing had been overheard by a girl that hadn't done anything wrong except be related to Mitch McIntyre, who was fast proving himself to be the most immature kid in our grade.

Rubbing the back of my head nervously, I replied, "I guess we did say some pretty vulgar things. And I see now that it was wrong." I paused and took her hand in mine. She looked down at our clasped hands and then looked into my eyes. "I'm sorry, Megs. That was a crap thing of us to do to you."

"No, it's not that. All adolescent boys are perverts. It's just... you were the only one that didn't say anything to objectify me. In fact, you were the one who told them enough was enough and changed the subject. I always admired you for that."

"Yeah, I guess I did."

"Why?" she asked. Megan took both my hands in hers and locked gazes. "Why would you defend me when we weren't even friends?"

"We're friends now," I said.

We gazed into one another's eyes and things

were really starting to heat up, and I guess I got nervous, because right when I thought she was leaning in to kiss me, I let go of her hands and started onward again.

"We're burning daylight," I said. "Best get moving."

Over my shoulder, I heard Megan chastising herself. "Stupid, stupid, stupid. He's just a kid for crying out loud."

After Billy, I was next to turn fifteen. Then Paul. And if Megan was sixteen going on seventeen like Sarah, our age gap wasn't even that bad. I mean, she'd technically be a senior when I was a sophomore. And senior guys dates sophomores and freshman girls all the time. Why couldn't a senior girl date a sophomore if she wanted? It was still a free country.

Anyway, I put it out of my mind, because as much as I loved Megan being a distraction, we had other matters to contend with. Like the one suddenly standing before us.

A soldier, missing the lower half of his right arm, stood across the street staring at us. Well, more specifically, staring at Megan.

Although his wound was bandaged, blood was

already seeping through the gauze wrap. He seemed to twist his tongue in his mouth and chew on it, a crooked grin forming on his mouth as he looked at us from behind a sunken and emotionless gaze.

"Hey, you kids shouldn't be wondering around out her on your own. You need to get to a shelter. The high school is fortified. I'll take you there."

"We're not going to the high school," I said.

"Oh, no?" the soldier asked. "And where, pray tell, might you be going?"

"We're looking for supplies," Megan interjected.

The soldier looked at her and licked his lips. A crooked grin slowly forming on his lips. "I hope you two ain't looting people's houses, because that's a crime."

"No," Megan said. "Nothing like that."

"Good," the soldier replied, his eyes fixed on her as he seemed to deliberately ignore me. It felt as if I didn't even exist.

"In that case, I should probably join you both. Make sure you stay safe. There's monsters roaming about."

"Oh, we know all about them," I said.

The soldiers piercing cold gaze snapped onto me

and he seemed to glare at me with unholy resentment, then he smiled and laughed. It was an artificial laugh. The kind you make when you're trying to humor somebody so that they'll like you. But it was clear this guy didn't like anyone but for maybe himself.

"You do, do you?" the soldier asked. He looked back at Megan. "Well, that's good, I suppose. So where are you two headed?"

"No place in particular," Megan said. She grabbed my hand and, giving me a gentle tug, added, "Come on, Travis. We best be going."

We began walking when the soldier jogged up next to us. He matched our pace and began to explain his situation. "My reserve unit was assigned Woodridge as one of the ground zeros for the meteor fallout. Turns out, there were a bunch of aliens that came along for the ride. Whether they're here intentionally or not, they proved to be dangerous. So, we were given orders to exterminate them. But they're far more elusive and vicious than we could have imagined. My entire unit was cut down. Heck, I didn't even come out of it unscathed."

He raised his bloody stump to show us then set it back down by his side. As we sped up, he continued to match our pace, not letting us pull away and sticking with us whether we wanted him to or not.

"So, what are you doing here?" I asked.

He shot me a cold look and then continued on, as if I'd never asked the question.

"I'm trying to find any survivors or other reserve units. If we can rally together, we might still have a fighting chance of taking these things down."

By now we'd walked almost two full blocks and I could tell Megan was growing more and more uncomfortable. Eventually, I stopped and said, "Well, we wish you the best of luck and thank you for your service."

"What'd you say to me?"

"I said, 'good luck'," I replied.

The soldier reached out and grabbed the collar of my shirt and drew me into him. "Look, you little punk. I don't need any damn luck. I've got skill in spades. And my number one skill is killing these alien scumbags. So, I don't need your condescending half-compliments."

"I wasn't…"

"It's all right," Megan interrupted. "We were just leaving anyway. Have a good day."

Megan grabbed my hand again and dragged me behind her as she marched up the street. This time it wasn't a gentle holding of hands but, rather, a let's get out of here with a kind of urgency in her step.

"Hey," the soldier laughed, jogging to catch up to us. "I can't let you two just wonder off on your own. You're a couple of kids."

"Look," Megan said, stopping mid-stride and spinning around to confront the soldier who was tailing us. "We didn't ask for your help. We certainly don't need it."

"No," he said with a chuckle, "I suppose you don't. But you will."

Without warning he grabbed her by her jersey with his good arm, jerked her toward him, and headbutted her. Megan sunk to her knees, her nose bleeding.

"What the hell," Megan mumbled, reaching up and touching the gash on the bridge of her split open nose.

"Get away from her!" I shouted. I charged forward and the soldier side-stepped my assault and hit me in the back of my neck with a well place karate chop.

The force of the hit was like nothing I'd ever felt before and I sank to my knees, holding the back of my neck, I winced from the pain. Before I could push myself back to my feet, the soldier turned and kicked me onto my side.

Instantly winded, I rolled over and clutched my gut, but before I could even try to breathe, the soldier walked up and kicked me while I was down. This time I thought that I might pass out from the blow, because my lungs couldn't open and my vision was fading due to a lack of oxygen.

My faced turned red as my lungs burned, but somehow I managed to roll over so I could better see Megan. I strained to see how she was doing, my neck taught with bulging veins as snot and tears streamed down my face.

"It seems," said the soldier, his eyes wild as he smiled at Megan with a grin full of malicious intent, "that your little boyfriend here doesn't have the guts to protect you."

"Screw you, asshole!" Megan shouted, spitting at the soldier. "He's more of a man than you'll ever be."

The soldiers eyes grew large with rage and he backhanded Megan, splitting open her lip to match her busted up nose. "It seems you need a lesson in respecting your elders, sweetheart."

"Elders?" Megan scoffed, wiping blood from her nose and lip with the back of her hand and smearing it across her right cheek. "What are you, like three years older than me?"

"Something like that," the soldier sneered. He walked casually up to Megan and, roughly grabbing her by the hair, kneed her right in the sternum. She fell back, landed on her side with a thud, and began coughing as she gagged on the blood already running down her swollen face.

Lying on her side, she grinned a bloody smile, spat, and growled, "Is that the best you got, you pussy?"

"Oh, you haven't had enough yet?" asked the soldier. He walked over to Megan and then, flipping her onto her stomach, tried to pull down her pants. She kicked and squirmed, and managed to break away, proving to be too wily for the handicapped soldier to get a proper hold on. "Hold still, you little bi—"

"Get away from her!" I screamed at the top of my lungs. Using all of my strength, I somehow managed to struggle to my feet.

The soldier paused his assault on Megan and put a hand to his ear, pretended to listen and then looked down at Megan. "Did you hear something? It sounded like a pesky little gnat. After I'm done with you, sweetheart, I think I'll squash that gnat too."

Realizing that this wasn't going to end well, for either of us, I did the stupidest thing I'd ever done in my life. Pushing through the pain, I charged the soldier full speed and tackled him.

We crashed to the ground, giving Megan time to stand up and grab her hockey stick, which had fallen off in the scuffle.

I beat the soldier to our feet but he abruptly swept my legs and knocked me back down again. The soldiers focus still on me, Megan used this chance to raise the hockey stick high above her and was about to strike the soldier across the head when he drew his gun on us.

Megan froze and then slowly backed up. "Look, man, we don't want any trouble."

"Oh, but you got it. Stepped right in it, didn'tcha?"

"Look, dude, we're not your enemy," I said. "There are real monsters out there." I pointed a finger down the street to emphasize my point, even though

I didn't know where the pack of roving aliens was at this time. But I would give anything for them to show up now and dispatch this A-hole.

"Oh, I know all about monsters," the soldier said. He pointed the gun at his own head and said, "They all live inside here, wouldn't you know?"

It was then that I realized the lights were on but nobody was home.

"Drop the stick," the soldier said, keeping his gun trained on Megan. He slowly rose up. When I shuffled, he focused his aim on me and said, "Don't move! I'm out of patience with both of you."

"Take it easy, Mr." Megan said. "We'll just get our things and be out of your hair. Promise."

"You promise me that, do you?"

"What is it you want?" I asked.

He looked as though he pondered it for a real second or two and then, a creepy grin spread across his wire-thin lips and he looked right at Megan. Wagging his gun at her, he replied, "I want *her*."

Walking up to Megan, he grabbed her by the wrist and pulled her up to her feet. Megan shoved him back and tried to turn and run but he cracked her in the back of her head with the butt of his gun and she crashed to the ground.

"Megs!" I cried out. Unable to stand up for fear of the soldier swatting me down again, I crawled over to her and rolled her over onto my lap and checked her pulse. She was out cold. Furious, I looked up and growled, "You son-of-a—"

"Let me stop you there, kid," the soldier said, wagging his gun at me, "before you say something you might regret."

"The only thing I regret," I said in my lowest, angriest voice, "is running into you."

"Oh, you're a comedian, I see. Well, I'm not amused." Sliding the gun across his chest, he used the friction to pull back the slide, cocked the gun, and then pointed it right at my head. "Any final prayers, smart ass?"

I closed my eyes but didn't have anything more to say to this psycho. Instead, and against my better judgement, I simply murmured, "Just get it over with."

"Fine," the one-armed soldier said in a detached manner that sent chills down my spine. "Have it your way."

There was a resounding *thunk*, like metal smashing against brick, and I cracked open one eye and peeked out to find Jimmy "Mad Dog" Polson holding a pipe as he stood over the soldier's unconscious body.

"Who's this one-armed asshole?" he asked.

"You have no idea how glad I am to see you, Jimmy," I said, slowly rising to my feet. Jimmy reached out and helped me the rest of the way up and then looked down at Megan.

"Is she all right?"

Megan groaned and stirred, which not only answered Jimmy's question but gave us both a huge sense of relief. Megan slowly sat up, touched her forehead, winced, and then asked, "What happened?"

"This prick," I said nodding at the soldier lying next to her, "knocked you out."

Megan looked up at me, then at Jimmy. I jutted a thumb in Jimmy's direction and said, "Jimmy showed up out of the blue and saved our sorry asses."

"Thanks, kid," she said, reaching up a hand. I took her hand in mine and helped her up. She paused, looked at me long and hard, and then said, "Oh, and Travis, one more thing."

"Yes?" I asked, looking into her beautiful blue eyes. She reached over, grabbed my neck, and drew me into her. Our lips crashed together and she kissed me long and hard, split lip and all.

"Woah!" Jimmy gasped. "Megan McIntyre is into you? I totally didn't see that one coming."

"Jimmy may have saved us, but you fought for me. You never stopped fighting. Not for an instant. And giving you a proper 'thank you' is the least I could do. You deserve it, and so much more."

"More?" I gulped. I didn't know what the insinuation was, but I liked the sound of 'more' whatever she meant by it.

"Don't stop on my account," Jimmy said as he bent over and picked up the soldier's gun while Megan and I locked lips a second time. He tucked it in the back of his pants waistband and then turned back toward us.

Megan and I made out for a hot minute, but Jimmy grew impatient with us and cleared his throat. When we didn't respond the first time, he cleared his throat again, but more loudly. We paused and looked over at him. "Yes?" asked Megan, slightly annoyed by the interruption. She wasn't done "thanking" me yet, and Jimmy was just a third wheel.

"Good. Now that you two are done tickling each

other's tonsils, what do you think we should do with this turd bag?" Jimmy tilted his head toward the soldier lying on the ground and waited for our answer.

"If we left him out here for the aliens to gut, it would serve him right," Megan said. I nodded in agreement.

"Wait a minute," I said, looking over at the dumpster over by the Lion's Club building. "I think I might have an idea."

Scooping the soldier up by his arms, I looked at Jimmy and said, "You get his feet and help me get him into that dumpster over there."

As we moved his body over to the dumpster, I was thankful that we were on the side of town that hadn't been demolished yet by all the fighting.

"I'll get the lid," Megan said, running ahead of us and opening the dumpster.

With a heave-ho, Jimmy and I tossed the soldier into the dumpster and then Megan shut it again.

Dusting off her hands, she turned toward us and said, "Good riddance."

"Now what?" Jimmy asked.

"Well, let's start by you telling us what you're doing wondering the town all by yourself."

"Oh, yeah, right," Jimmy said, remembering what it was he had come here to do. "I was looking for you guys. My parents… actually, all of the parents… even Ms. Carol and your mom, too… are all dug in at the high school. The military is bussing people out of town as we speak. I guess the aliens are a bit too much for them to handle. It's a full on evacuation."

"We've got to tell the others," Megan said.

"Come on," I said, grabbing Megan's hand as the three of us jogged up the street, racing toward Fort Liberty to warn our friends. "There's no time to lose."

Almost as soon as we had begun to find a steady pace, the emergency tornado sirens began to blare all across Woodridge. Sirens blaring meant one thing and one thing only—imminent attack.

# 6

## INVASION
### PART 6: ALL THE ADULTS ARE GONE NOW

**B**Y THE TIME WE RETURNED TO FORT LIBERTY, told everyone what was going on, packed up our things, and trekked all the way back across town without a single encounter with an alien, we arrived at an empty high school parking lot.

Eerily, there were no buses, no soldiers, no people, and, for that matter, not a single sign of our parents. To make matters worse, the gates had been left wide open. It was as if they had up and abandoned their homes, leaving without a trace.

"It just doesn't make any sense," Jimmy said. "They had armed guards at the gate." He pointed at the gate, then spun around and pointed at the rooftop. "And they had spot lights on the roof to drive the aliens away, too."

"There's nothing up there," Paul observed.

"I can see that, now," Jimmy said.

"What else can you remember," I asked. "Does anything stick out to you?"

"I mean, there was chatter that the aliens were mainly hovering around the old power plant, for some reason."

"The power plant?" asked Megan. "Isn't the old power plant nuclear?"

"I think so," I replied.

"Anyway," Jimmy continued, "the buses were already being loaded with the survivors and their families when I left. But there were too many people to evacuate in that amount of time."

"So, where did they all go?" Mitch asked, scratching his head.

All of us were puzzled. But then Melody broke the silence.

"They left us," she said. "They left us all here to die."

"No," I said, shaking my head. "Mom wouldn't do that." Melody ran up to me, her eyes brimming with tears, and latched onto me. I hugged her and let her sob into my chest.

"I hate to admit it," Paul said, "But I think Trav's sis might be right. They left us."

"That can't be right," Jimmy said. "My mom said she'd wait for me."

"Maybe something else happened to them," Paul stated. "Something that forced them to push up the evacuation timeline."

"The aliens, perhaps?" Billy suggested, thinking aloud. But he knew as well as we did that, just by looking around, there were no signs of a skirmish.

"There's no blood, or bodies, or claw marks," Sarah said, looking around.

"Look, no matter how you want to sugar coat it, we're here and they're not. Call it what you will, but it looks like they abandoned us," Mitch said. "Got out while they still could. I mean, who could blame them?"

"Hey," Jimmy said angrily, pressing a finger into Mitch's chest. "Maybe your family would up and leave you, but my mom wouldn't just leave me. She wouldn't."

"Sorry," Mitch said, taking a step back. "I didn't mean it like that... all I meant was..."

"Look," I said, trying to diffuse the tension best I knew how. "We can't pretend to know what went on here, but our moms said to come here if things got any worse, and I think we can all agree things have gotten pretty damn bad. So, let's shut these gates and see if there's anything we can scavenge for around here."

Billy reached into his bag and pulled out some chains and wrapped them around the gate to ensure that it wouldn't be easily opened. "This should keep everything out short of a tank."

"Do you always carry chains around with you wherever you go?" Jimmy asked, looking down and eyeing Billy's bag with curiosity.

"I just grabbed things I thought we might need." Then, pointing at the gate, he added, "And I was right."

Jimmy patted Billy on the back. "Good job, Back Woods Bardem. You always come through in a pinch."

"I try." Billy chuckled, bent down, and picked up his bag. Tossing it across his shoulder, he pointed at the high school. "Let's head inside."

"I'm going to raid the fridge in the teacher's lounge," Paul said. "They always have food in there."

"And soda," Mitch added.

"Lead the way, fat-ass," Jimmy said, gesturing for

Mitch to lead the way.

"Hey, sis, you gonna let this punk talk to your baby brother like that?" Mitch turned toward Megan who just blinked and stared blankly at him.

"Well, considering he saved my life, I think he can say whatever he wants."

"Thank you," Jimmy said, smiling at Megan. "See, even your hot sister agrees with me."

"My sister isn't hot, you idiot," Mitch fired back. "She's, at best, a two."

"Oh, yeah? Try telling that to Travis."

"What's that supposed to mean?"

"Well, they were playing tonsil tag earlier. So, obviously Travis also thinks Megan is pretty hot. Otherwise, why would he let her stick her tongue down his throat, huh, wise guy? Answer me that."

"You lie!" Mitch shouted back. "Besides, my dog licks my face all the time. Doesn't mean I like making out with my dog."

"Keep telling yourself that," Jimmy retorted. "But I ain't lying."

Mitch turned to me and said, "Come on, Trav. Don't let him start rumors like that."

"Like what?" asked Megan. "Like this?" She then

strolled up to me, ran her fingers through the back of my hair, and then kissed me long and good right in front of everyone.

Mitch staggered backward, hardly able to believe his eyes. "No, this can't be happening."

"Oh, it's happening," Megan assured him.

"I thought you said he was your disgusting brothers little friend," Sarah said, stepping in and separating us with a gentle press of her hand against my chest. "And mentioned to my face, I might add, that it would be gross to lock lips with such an immature, inexperienced, freshman?"

"A girl can change her mind, can't she? Besides, Travis is my knight in shining armor. He threw himself into harm's way to protect me. He made sure I was okay after being attacked. So what if I want to repay his kindness with a little bit of my own?"

"Look, it's not like we're dating," I said, trying to comfort and obviously distraught Mitch. "I mean, would I date your sister? Sure. She's drop-dead gorgeous. Even if you don't see it, the rest of us do. And is she a good kisser? Based on my limited experience, I'd say, yes. Do I want to kiss her again? I could kiss your sister all day long. Her lips are like heavenly nectar and—"

"Let me cut you off there, sweetie," Megan said, putting her arm around me and drawing me into her. "But you're not helping."

"Uh, yeah. Right. It's just that I really, really like you."

"Oh, you're so sweet!" she said, bopping my nose with her finger and acting all lovey-dovey."

Mitch stewed in his anger and we all watched as his left eye began to twitch.

"Are you going to be alright, man?" Paul asked, waving his hand in front of Mitch's face.

Mitch slapped his hand away and then fritzed out, spasming, and waving his arms all about as though he were chasing away a swarm of bees.

"Get off of me," he growled. Stopping after a few steps, he turned and pointed an angry finger at me. "I thought you were my friend. But now I see you for what you really are. A no good, sister-humping, back stabber."

We watched Mitch march up to the school doors and check them. He rattled the crossbar handle, but it was clearly locked. Then, looking around, he found a cinderblock lying nearby and used it to smash the entrance window.

Reaching in through the opening, Mitch unlatched the lock and opened the door. Turning around, he looked at all of us and said, "Well, it's open. So…"

"Yeah, buddy. We can see that," Paul said. Paul was the first one to go on inside, followed by my sister, Billy, Sarah and Megan. Megan paused and looked at Mitch, but she didn't say anything. It was her life, not his. So, he could butt out as far as she was concerned.

Everyone went on inside, but I held back to talk to Mitch who was holding the door for everyone.

"Will you be okay?" I asked.

He looked at me, paused as though he were going to say something, then turned his face away. "I don't talk to traitors," he informed me.

"Look, it wasn't like I was pursuing your sister. It just sort of happened."

"Oh, so your tongue just accidentally slipped out of your head and into her mouth?"

"Dude, it's not like that." I paused briefly and shook my head. "No, actually, it was exactly like that."

"Greeeat," he replied, sarcastically.

"Look, I like Megs," I said. "I'm not going to deny

it. She's great. So, if we get married, you'll be my brother-in-law."

"Brothers?" Mitch asked, his gaze slowly turning back to me.

"Hell, yeah. Brothers," I repeated, holding out my fist and offering a fist bump.

A smile broke across Mitch's face and his look of betrayal and disappointment melted away. "Brothers!" he said, growing excited at the prospect.

Finally, Mitch gave in and we bumped fists. "Brothers," I said, putting a definitive end to our spat.

We both headed inside and Mitch caught up to everyone else when I spotted Megan hanging back by the drinking fountain as she waited for me.

She leaned against the wall by the fountain and smiled at me. "So, you like me, huh?"

"You heard all that, did you?"

"I'm sorry for eavesdropping. I just didn't want my brother acting like he's my keeper. He's not. I can make my own decisions."

"I know you can."

"But," she said, clasping her arms behind her back and leaning forward so that her chest was in my line of sight, "I also like being taken care of." She stood up and twirled once in the hallway and then laughed. "Jimmy may have technically saved our lives, but you were throwing yourself at a deranged man to protect me. That's the most noble thing I've ever seen, Travis Mahoney."

"Great?" I said, half questioning what it was we were even talking about. "So, are we… I mean, we've kissed twice, so, like, are we… you know…"

"Dating?" she asked, finishing my thought for me. I nodded.

She thought about it for a moment and then shook her head. "I don't know, Trav. I like you, but you're still just a pup. How about this… we take it slow, let things unfold naturally, and see how it goes. No pressure to commit, or try to be something you're not, just let it happen however it happens. Does that sound like a plan?"

"I mean, I've never had a girlfriend before. So, I don't know what I'm doing anyway. So, I guess?"

Megan laughed and then walked up to me and stopped directly in front of me. We stared at each other for what seemed like ages and then she threw her arms around me and gave me the biggest, warmest embrace of my life.

"Jeez," a voice called out. "Get a room you two!"

We turned to see Melody and Billy standing in the hallway watching us. Obviously, my sister still felt she was the comedian of the group.

"We were just coming to check and see if everything was all right. But if you need some more time…" Billy thumbed over his shoulder and said, "We can leave you two alone."

"No," Megan replied. "We're good."

"Yeah," I answered. "We're good."

"Good, I'm glad we're all good," Melody quipped. "Now, if you'd be so kind as to get your butts to the teacher's lounge, somebody left an entire pepperoni pizza in the fridge."

"Pizza?" I asked, my stomach growling.

Megan looked down at me and laughed. "I can't remember the last time we had anything to eat, can you?"

I shook my head. She grabbed my hand and started up the hallway. Billy and my sister followed after us.

Once we arrived at the teacher's lounge, everyone hooted and hollered and whistled at Megan and I.

"I hope you used protection," Jimmy said,

between bites of a slice of pepperoni.

"Shut up, dickhole," Megan snapped.

Jimmy raised a hand and backed off, taking another bite of his pizza. Mouth full, he replied, "Sorry, was just trying to lighten the mood."

Megan pointed a finger at everyone. "I know I was maybe a bit of a hypocrite saying I'd never date any of my brothers little friends. Well, I'll own up to that. But don't you dare think for a minute that I'd let anyone make Travis feel less than for liking me."

"She's right," Sarah added. "Technically, you're all officially Freshman now. High school upperclassman date underclassman all the time. In fact, it's almost to be expected."

Everything settled down as we sat around the table enjoying the pizza. After several minutes of eating together in silence, it was my little sister who was the first to break the quiet.

"Uh, guys," Melody said. She was standing by the windows, looking out onto the football field. "Maybe we should find somewhere else to stay for the night."

"What are you talking about?" asked Billy. He walked up to the window and stood beside her. His smile vanished and we could tell by the serious look that took its place, something wasn't right.

"What is it?" I asked.

Soon enough, we all joined her and peered out of the faculty breakroom windows. What we saw didn't exactly fill us with hope.

Piled into one giant heap in the back of the school athletic field was a mound of bodies. Human bodies.

"There was no time to dig a mass grave," Paul said. "So, the military just piled all the dead bodies here."

"I don't want to be here anymore," Melody said, burying her face in her arm and crying. Sarah dropped to one knee and hugged Melody.

"Don't worry, Mel, it'll be all right."

"I think I see old Mrs. Lancaster from church," Mitch said, squinting at one of the bodies in the pile. "Yeah, over there. That's her walker."

"Don't point them out," Billy said.

"What should we do, Billy?" asked Jimmy. "Should we bury them?"

"That many?" I asked. "Without a shovel loader and a bag of lime, that would be impossible."

"Lime?" Melody asked.

"It's that white powder you see in war movies or

films about the holocaust that they dump on mass graves," Paul informed. "It helps prevent purification."

"Travis is right. Right now, there's nothing we can do," Megan said. "We'll have to leave them there."

"But who killed them all?" Melody asked.

We all turned and looked outside. The bodies weren't torn to shreds by the aliens, but there were bullet wounds. A lot of them. None of us wanted to admit it, but it looked like there hadn't been enough room on the buses and, well, it was too terrible to think about.

"We don't know," I answered. I shot Megan a look that she also shared. Although we didn't know for certain what had gone down, we had a pretty good idea.

Perhaps there weren't enough seats. Maybe they drew lots to see who'd get the seats. It's possible they loaded as many as they could onto the buses and then someone who hadn't been selected decided that they weren't going to get left behind.

Staring out at the bodies, I'm fairly sure we all imagined similar scenarios. Determined not to get left behind, a mob charged the buses. The soldiers did what soldiers are trained to do. And, now, there was a massive pile of decomposing bodies stacked behind the school.

As I stood looking out, I couldn't help be stunned at how fast everything fell apart all around us. It only took three days for the aliens to overrun the town. In that time, the military went with a shock and awe tactic that hadn't been used since Vietnam in a desperate attempt to quell the alien incursion. And I couldn't help but feel that if it was this way all across the country, then we were in for a long, hard ride.

"The sun will be going down, soon," Billy said, looking up at the dusk laden sky. "And even if we were to get back to Fort Liberty safely, all the supplies are on this side of town. The remaining side of town. So, it only makes sense to hunker down here, tonight."

"Also, the home ec room has a couple of sofas we can sleep on and gas stoves we can light if we're cold," Megan said. "We could boil a big pot of water, keep the heat for the night."

"And the locker rooms have showers," Sarah added. "And the boiler room is still on, so we'll have hot water."

"No co-ed showers," Mitch said. He pointed at me and then Billy. "As a pastor's son, I need to inform you that just because you two have girlfriends now at the end of the world doesn't mean you can get away with any twisted hanky-panky."

"No end of the world hanky-panky," Billy said, shooting me a wry grin. "Got it."

I hid a smile and turned away so as not to offend Mitch who was being entirely serious.

"You always need to remind us that you're the son of a pastor, don't you?" Jimmy said. "It's like you think you're better than us just because your dad makes a living talking to an imaginary man in the sky!"

"God isn't imaginary!" Mitch fired back.

"Oh, yeah?" Jimmy asked. He pointed out the window. "Tell that to the pile of dead bodies out there. Where was your God when they were all dying?"

"Guys, guys!" Sarah said, stepping in-between them and raising her hands to keep them separated if they decided to go at it. "As much as we all love a good theological debate, now is not the time or place."

Jimmy folded his arms across his chest and huffed angrily to himself. Mitch threw his arms up and walked away. "I can't deal with this now."

"We're all tired, a little bit dirty, and we haven't had any good sleep in days. The stress of it all is finally wearing on us. So, my suggestion," I said, "We get clean. We get cozy. And we lock ourselves in for the night."

"Travis speaks words of wisdom," Billy said. "And I fully agree. Tonight, we rest."

"What do we do tomorrow?" Melody scanned all of our faces looking for answers. Naturally, it fell to Billy to think of what to say.

"Tomorrow we're going to visit every single one of our houses and look for our parents. If anyone is still alive out there, we're going to find them."

That was a great answer, I thought. It satisfied everyone's concerns and gave us a mission of hope that we could all look forward to. Our stress melted away and we all headed to the locker rooms to lather up and scrub down.

On the way to the locker rooms, Lucy came around the corner. Although it didn't startle us, we'd forgotten that Jimmy didn't know about her being friendly now.

"Watch out!" Jimmy shouted, drawing the gun he'd taken off of the crazed soldier.

"No!" I shouted. I jumped in front of Jimmy and grabbed the gun, raising it above our heads just as the gun went off.

"What are you doing?!" Jimmy shouted. "One of the aliens has infiltrated the school."

"It's a friendly," I shouted.

Jimmy took a step back and then leaned to the side and looked over my shoulder to see the alien sitting in the middle of the Hallway with Megan, Melody, Mitch, and Paul standing in front of it as they formed a human shield to protect Lucy.

"Its name is Lucy," Melody said.

"Lucy?" Jimmy repeated, still dazed and confused. "What are you guys talking about?" He pointed a finger at Lucy. "That's an alien!"

"It's a friendly alien," Billy said, walking up to us. He held out his hand, inching cautiously closer, and said, "I know it's a lot to take in, but I need you to give me the gun, Jimmy."

"Hell, no!" Jimmy protested, drawing back. "Nobody is getting this gun off of me unless it's over my dead body."

Sarah stepped toward Jimmy from his left, as she, Billy, and I slowly encircled him. Jimmy stepped back again, his back up against the wall.

"Just give us the gun, Jimmy," Sarah said,

cautiously raising her hands as she inched closer toward him. Still, he refused.

"Screw that," he said, taking another step back.

Sarah held out her hand, "Give it over."

"No," he replied, doubling down. "If that thing comes near me, I'm blasting it."

"This tactic doesn't seem to be working," I whispered out of the corner of my mouth.

Sarah looked back at Billy and I and then she did the bravest, most selfless thing any of us had ever done in the face of someone wielding a deadly weapon. She offered herself up as a sacrifice.

"How about this... If I show you my boobs, Jimmy, will you hand over the gun then?"

"Heck, yeah!" Jimmy replied. He spun the gun around in his palm without so much as a moment's hesitation, and hand it off to her. She took it, handed it off to Billy, and then faced Jimmy again.

Her back to all of us, we watched Jimmy's eyes light up as Sarah Lewis, the hottest cheerleader in all of Woodridge High, lifted up her uniform and flashed him.

Sarah put her shirt back down, tucked her uniform back into her skirt as she turned back around and approached us. "And that's how you handle a successful peace negotiation," she said.

Billy stuffed the gun in his bag and, at the same time, we both looked over at Jimmy. A stupid grin spread ear to ear and he held up two giant thumbs up.

"Holy cow, you're all a bunch of iditols," Melody said, letting loose and overdramatic sigh. "Come on, Lucy. We're leaving these perverts and finding a nice spot to sleep.

# 7

## INVASION
### PART 7: THE THING THAT FELL TO EARTH

ONCE THE GUN HAD BEEN STOWED AND THE drama was over, we made our way to the homemaking classroom. Not having been this deep into the high school before, we were pleasantly surprised to find that the girls hadn't been lying. The home economics teacher was "cozy obsessed," to put it mildly.

Numerous pieces of furniture populated the classroom. Off to the corner of the room, behind a row of stoves, there was a nook with an old La-Z Boy armchair that you'd find in someone's living room, and a love seat in sat next to a full-sized sofa. There were even three beanbag chairs. And for the cherry on top, hanging on the wall was a sign that read "Lazy Corner."

Not only was this room safe and secure, but we had enough places for all of us to sleep. It would be like a giant slumber party or a lock-in with friends and classmates of varying age and grade.

Exhausted from another long day of trekking across town, not to mention the whole ordeal with the gun and the added stress that brought, Melody was the first to find a blanket and curl up on the love sofa. Lucy, the alien monster, sat down on the floor beside her and kept his eye on the door, like a loyal watchdog protecting its owner.

Paul, Mitch, and Jimmy plopped themselves down on the Persian styled rug that brought Cozy Corner together and made themselves comfortable. Reaching into his jacket, Mitch drew out a pack of playing cards and all three started a game of five-card stud while Sarah and Megan prepared to go take showers.

Meanwhile, as everyone split off to do different things, Billy and I just perusing the cupboards and pantries, looking for snacks. Of course, it being a school, there weren't any. But we did find some teabags and put on a couple of kettles.

"I really hate tea," Jimmy said.

"Well, then you don't have to drink it," Mitch replied.

"Coffee is even worse," Paul added, making a sour face.

"I actually like coffee," I said.

"Will you dorks shut up?" Melody said, raising her head and shooting us all an upset glare. "Some people are trying to get their beauty sleep."

"Sorry," Billy answered. "We'll try to keep it down."

Melody yawned and put her head back down, using the sofa cushion as a pillow.

"You kids behave while Megan and I are away," Sarah said. We smiled and watched them leave. Megan paused in the entrance and turned to blow me a kiss just before the door swung shut.

"Megan and Travis, sitting in a tree, K-I-S-S-I-N-G. First comes love, then comes marriage, then comes the baby in the baby carriage." Jimmy laughed at his own lame joke and went back to playing cards.

"So, what do you think two girls like that get up to in the same shower?" Paul looked up when there was no answer and scanned our faces.

"Nothing," Mitch answered. "Because, A, the

girl's showers have curtains in them, unlike in the boys locker rooms. And, B, that's my sister. And it's gross to think about."

"I bet they're lathering up with a bar of soap and scrubbing each other down," Jimmy blurted out.

"Yeah," Paul said, pointing at Jimmy. "That's what I'm talking about!"

They high-fived one another and went back to focusing on the card game.

"Guys, guys!" Billy said. He gestured toward me and then himself. "Those are our girlfriends you're talking about. Show some respect."

"Sorry, Billy," Jimmy said in a facetious manner that was only half sincere.

Billy and I looked at one another and then he pulled two bath towels out of his bag and handed me one. "Here," he said. "You'll need it for after your shower."

"What don't you have in there?" I asked.

Billy laughed. "Come on, we best take a quick rinse." He raised his arm and sniffed his own armpit and then recoiled. "Dude, why didn't anyone tell me I was this ripe?"

Mitch shrugged. "Maybe because you're the one

getting all the action."

"That's not true," Billy replied. "Travis and your sister are…"

"No," Mitch said cutting him off. "Travis is a complete gentleman and would never take advantage of my sister. Not in that way."

"That's a total lie," Jimmy said. "They were making out right in front of me. She wants him bad, I can tell."

"And it's perfectly fine, because once they're married then they won't make God sad anymore with their hedonistic ways."

Jimmy didn't know how to respond to that and he merely looked up at me and said, "Hear that, Travis? You make God sad."

I laughed but then quickly pretended to cough.

"Nice cover," Billy whispered, sticking his hand up so that Mitch wouldn't see his lips moving.

"I totally can hear you, bro.," Mitch said without looking up from his cards.

Billy shrugged and then he and I left the others to go shower. On the way to the locker room, we passed the girls who had already finished washing and were on their way back to Cozy Corner.

They had wet hair and glistening skin, and their faces were rosy from the after-warmth of a nice hot shower, so we knew they had washed.

"That was quick," I said.

"Yeah, well. There's not much to do other than get clean," Megan said.

"See you soon?" I asked.

"You bet. And you can sleep next to me tonight," she replied. "I mean, if you want to."

She sounded as nervous as I felt, but I replied, "Okay. Sure, why not?"

"Same for you, slugger," Sarah said, lightly punching Billy's shoulder.

"You want me to sleep with Megan too?"

"No, silly," Sarah answered, laughing aloud. "Not her… I meant, with me."

"Oh, yeah," Billy said, blushing and feeling stupid. "That makes more sense."

"You think?"

"Catch you ladies, later," I said.

After saying our goodbyes, Billy and I took the longest shower of our lives. If I were to guess precisely how long, I'd say that it must have been forty-five minutes or more, because we steamed up the whole of the boys' locker room.

Billy and I barely spoke a word the entire time. To be completely honest, we had too many things going on in our heads to speak. We just let the steam engulf us in a shroud of white, and we used the soap and lathered our bodies not once, not twice, but three times just for good measure.

Once we were satisfied we were squeaky clean and that any B.O. from the past few days had been swiftly washed down the drain, we dressed and headed back to the home ec room.

When we returned, everyone was already asleep. Megan and Sarah had also fallen fast asleep and were spooning on the big sofa while Mitch took the La-Z Boy, and Paul and Jimmy had the beanbag chairs. That only left one beanbag chair and a blanket for Billy and me to share.

Billy and I looked at one another and we both laughed. "Shall we?" he said, gesturing to the beanbag chair. I nodded and we tried to settle down onto the beanbag at the same time. But it proved more difficult to do than either of us had anticipated.

"It's a tight fit," he said shifting his weight to try and get comfortable.

Of course, whenever he shifted, the bag would bump me off and whenever I hopped back on, Billy would slide off the other end.

"This thing is tricky," I grumbled, trying to find the right balance so he and I could sleep on the beanbag chair together.

"No kidding," he said, shifting again. And, again, I rolled off the opposite side.

Finally, I gave up and stood up. "You can have it," I said, letting Billy keep the beanbag chair. "I'll sleep over here on the floor.

"You sure?"

"Yeah. It's fine."

"Thanks, Trav," he said, and curled up and went to sleep.

I took the flimsy blanket and went and laid down on the rug. It may have been the worst rug I've ever had the displeasure to lie down on. The wear and tear of a thousand feet a day had really done a number on it, and it was grimy and riddled with holes. As I pulled the blanket over me, I glanced around and noticed that everyone had gone to sleep except for me and Lucy.

When I looked over at Lucy, he was just staring at me with all six eyes. I didn't know what to make of it other than, for whatever reason, I felt a deep calm come over me. "Go to sleep, Lucy," I said. "It's okay."

Lucy seemed to acknowledge my words and stretched out and rolled onto its side. A few more minutes past and, for whatever reason, I still couldn't fall asleep.

*"Pssst!"* a voice whispered. "Travis, you still awake?"

I looked over to find Megan sitting in the middle of the sofa staring at me. She shoved Sarah to the side and patted the sofa cushion next to her, offering me a spot on the couch.

"Come here, Travis," she said. "That floor looks really uncomfortable. Come, sleep next to me."

She wasn't wrong. The floor was actually quite miserable. Picking myself up, I went and cozied up on the couch beside her. "Thanks," I said.

Megan gently pushed me down so that my head was resting on her arm and then she curled herself around me. Wrapping her arms around my body, she put her head next to mine, touching her forehead to the back of my head.

"You're welcome," she replied. "And thank you, for having my back today. I really appreciated it."

"No problem," I replied. "It was my pleasure."

"Oh, and one more thing," she added, interrupting herself with a sleepy yawn. "You're a good kisser. I just wanted to tell you that."

Just then, Mitch let one rip in his sleep. His fart was so loud that Megan and I had to choke back a fit of laugher. Giggling softly, she said, "See what I mean?"

"Yeah," I replied. We laughed again and enjoyed the relaxing comfort of each other's warmth.

Not even three minutes later, Megan drifted off to sleep, her arms wrapped around me as she made me the little spoon; which I didn't mind in the slightest.

Light snoring filled the room and I slowly drifted off to sleep in Megan's arms. "Goodnight, Megs," I whispered, before succumbing to sleep.

"'Night, Trav," she whispered back, dreamily.

I don't remember much after that, because the Sandman came and I went out like a lightbulb.

The night wore on and before I realized it, the morning had returned and the first break of sunlight washed over me, arousing me from my slumber. As I slowly cracked my eyes open, I saw a blurry figure sitting across from the sofa. I reached up, rubbed my eyes and looked again. *Oh, for Heaven's sake. Not him again,* I thought, as the figure came into focus.

"Well, ain't this the sweetest thing you ever did see," a voice proclaimed. Everyone startled awake and sat up. They all looked over at what I was already staring at. Sitting before us, decked out in army green camo, was the one-armed soldier from yesterday.

He crouched in the middle of the room and, to our disappointment, he had found his gun.

"Who are you?" asked Paul, covering a yawn.

Brandishing his weapon, and waving it about menacingly, the soldier looked at Megs, me, and Jimmy and replied, "Why don't you ask your three little friends here, Larry, Curly, and Moe." The disdain in his voice was palpable, and Megan sat up and glared at him.

"What are you doing here?" Megan demanded to know, not letting him talk his way out of this one.

"Oh, I was just in the neighborhood and thought I'd settle in here for the night. Imagine my surprise when I found the little punks who'd knocked me unconscious, stole my gun, and dropped me into the nearest dumpster as if I were a piece of trash."

"You are a piece of trash," Jimmy replied.

"SHUT UP!" the soldier yelled, silencing the debate. "If I wanted to hear your opinion, I'd ask for it. But since I didn't…" He paused, took a deep breath and closed his eyes.

"What do you want?" asked Billy, slowly sitting forward in the beanbag chair.

"Uth-uh," the soldier said, shaking his head. Pressing the muzzle of his gun onto the floor, he pushed himself up with his good arm and then aimed the gun directly at Billy, urging Billy to relax. "Sit back down, kid. Just ask your friend there what happens to heroes who get overzealous." He looked right at me and smiled.

"What's he talking about, Travis?" Sarah asked, looking over at me.

"This A-hole is the one who beat me up and tried to have his way with Megan."

"That was you?" Billy asked, standing up. Billy took two steps toward the soldier but was abruptly cut short when the soldier raised his gun and pressed it into Billy's forehead.

"So, what if it was? What are you going to do about it?"

Billy didn't say anything but just glared at the

man.

"Look, I don't know what your damage is," Mitch said, "but we haven't done anything to you."

"Because he's a psycho," Megan said. Her words were chilling on several levels because she had hit the nail on the head. This guy was a nutcase.

"There she is!" the soldier said, turning and smiling at Megan. "There's my girl."

"Hit a nerve, did I?" Megan asked in a jeering manner that seemed to anger the soldier even more. The proof was in the fact that his face had suddenly turned two additional shades of red.

I stood up and blocked the soldier's view of Megan to run interference, since it seemed like he could only focus on one thing at a time. As I did, I saw my sister, Melody, quietly enter the room. She came in directly behind the soldier without his knowing, Lucy steadfast by her side. This gave me an idea.

"How about you tuck your little tail between your legs, and skedaddle."

"What are you doing, Trav?" Megan asked out of the corner of her mouth.

"Trust me," I whispered.

"Oh, the valiant boyfriend." The soldier tapped

the gun on his head, as if he were thinking about something, and after a brief pause, said, "I've been meaning to ask, ain't he a little too young for you?" He leaned to the side and looked directly at Megan. I moved a step over to block his view again and he huffed in an amused tone.

Megan scowled at him. "My love life is none of your business, pal. Besides, who do you think you are? You act all self-important, but for all we know you're a deserter."

"What'd you call me?" the soldier growled. His postured stiffened and he raised his gun, this time pointing it at Megan. Again, I stepped in front, blocking his line of sight.

"He, dickhead!" I said. This got his attention as his eyes shifted toward me and then, as predicted, the gun followed. "Does pulling a gun on a bunch of kids make you feel tough? Why are you even bothering us? Are you some kind of bully that never graduated Asshole school so you could never get a life? Why don't you stow your weapon and go crawl back under whatever rock it is you stepped out from... you knuckle-dragging, sister-humping, army-defecting, yellow-bellied, mouth-breather."

"Oh, snap!" Paul said. "My boy's got game."

The soldier tapped the barrel of his gun on his head and acted all crazy. Then he looked at me and said, "Give me one good reason why I shouldn't shoot you here and now?"

"Because you're already dead," I answered.

"I'm what?" the soldier laughed. "I think you're confused, kid." He trained his gun on me, his finger sliding down onto the trigger.

"No," I said, nodding my head at something just beyond his shoulder. "Over there."

"Yeah, like I'd fall for a trick like that."

"My brother is right," a small voice said. The soldier spun around to see my lil' sis standing in the doorway with Lucy by her side. Having a grizzly bear sized alien which towered over a twelve year old girl even while sitting, caused the soldier to take a giant step back.

Cool as a cucumber, Melody raised her little finger, pointed it at the soldier, and said to Lucy, "Sick 'em, boy."

Lucy, the thing that fell to Earth from outer space, leapt into the air and pounced onto the soldier, knocking him to the ground before he could get off a shot. The gun was knocked out of his hand and slid across the floor where it got caught under the toe of a boot. Standing over the weapon was none other than Billy "Backwoods" Bardem.

Casually, Billy bent down, picked up the weapon, racked it three times to make sure it was disengaged, and secured it in his waistband.

I walked up to Lucy, cautious and slow. Then, I crouched down next to her and looked at the soldier who was struggling to breath under the weight of the alien creature.

"I'm sorry you're damaged, man. Really, I am. But these are my friends. My family. And I'll do anything to protect them. You should have left when you had the chance. But you just had to stir the pot, didn't you?"

"Come on, kid," the soldier pleaded. "Give me a second chance. I can do better. I will do better."

I peered into his hollow eyes and shook my head, no. "I'm sorry, but you tried to hurt me and my friends. You assaulted my girlfriend. You pulled a gun on us. I think maybe the best thing for you to do is just stop existing."

"Wait, wait, please, just wait. I can explain..."

I stood back up and then took several large steps back. "Lucy, take this human garbage out and dispose of him."

Lucy looked up at me, fully understanding what I had said, and drug the soldier clawing and screaming down the school hallway.

"Oh, crap!" Paul shouted. "Lucy is actually going to deal with him. I've got to see this!"

He wasn't the only one who shared that sentiment. We all ran to the window and watched as Lucy flipped open the lid of the dumpster with one of his six tails, the other five hoisting the soldier into the air, and then dropping him into the dumpster.

The lid slammed shut again and Lucy turned and looked at us all. There was a pause and then all of his six tails started to glow, the ends flared out like arrow heads, and they all whipped about—piercing the metal dumpster. They put so many holes in the thing that it looked like Swiss cheese by the time Lucy was done.

"Ooh," Paul said, wincing at the thought of those barbed tails piercing a person's body. "Ouch."

"That's gotta sting," Jimmy said.

"I didn't tell him to do that," I said.

"No, but I did," Melody said, pressing her tiny face

up against the window. "Lucy is special," Melody continued, "because he can read my mind."

We all looked at her and then back out at the blood oozing out of the holes of the dumpster.

"It's wrong to kill," Mitch said.

"And I didn't kill him," Melody said. "Lucy did." She smiled and then skipped away, gleefully.

Mitch turned to me and said, "I think your sister might be a sociopath."

"No," I said. "It was the right call. That soldier wasn't going to leave us alone. He was wrong in the head."

Mitch took a step back and looked at us all with utter dismay and shock. "Are you people freaking insane?" He pointed out at the window. "That was a human life, we're talking about."

"He was going to shoot Travis and hurt all of us," Megan said, stepping up and defending what was, by all likelihood, the most strategic thing to do in order to guarantee all of our safety. "Maybe even worse."

Megan looked at Sarah who nodded in acknowledgement, knowing, as only women do, what kinds of torment can be worse than a quick death.

"Don't get all bent out of shape," Paul said. "The

guy was obviously insane."

"So, you just let him be killed? You didn't try to help him any other way?"

Billy stepped forward. "Mitch, look, it's not like that. It was a necessary call." He held up the gun. "See this? He had the safety turned off. You don't turn the safety off unless you intend to pull the trigger. And he was aiming it at my best friend. So, if it came down to it, who do you wish it would have been? That asshole out there, or Travis?"

"I don't believe you people. You're all justifying murder here. Do you realize that? It's beyond the pale. You know what… I'm done. I'm outa' here."

Mitch grabbed his jacket, pulled it on, and stormed out.

"Hey, man," Paul said, "Where you going?"

"Away from all of you," Mitch said, still furious.

I started to follow after him but Megan reached up and grabbed me by the shoulder and stopped me.

"It's probably better if you give him time to process. He's always looked up to our father, because our father honors things like family, God, and church. Mitch has always wanted to follow in our fathers footsteps and become a preacher someday. So, right now he's grappling with a very real moral problem that he can't easily unpack."

"You don't seem to be bothered by it," Jimmy said. "You two have the same father."

"I'm sure if the soldier busted up my brother's nose and told him he was going to have his way with him, Mitch would be singing a different tune. But since I was the one who was assaulted and threatened, I really don't give to figs about that ass-hat getting harpooned by an alien from another planet. Serves him right, as far as I'm concerned."

"Please don't take this the wrong way," Sarah said, stepping in and taking Megan's hand and squeezing it in solidarity and support. "But Mitch still has a lot of growing up to do. All of you are maturing at a faster rate, and that's fine. But when you have the mind of a child, sometimes the world just doesn't make sense."

"So, let me see if I understand you, but what you're saying is… we're more mature than Mitch?" asked Paul. "Even Jimmy?"

Sarah laughed. "Yes, even Jimmy."

Jimmy clicked his tongue and winked at Sarah, and nodded his head as if to say, "That's what I'm talking about."

Sarah rolled her eyes and then looked back at Paul. "But I may have to take that back."

"What?" Jimmy protested. "There's no takesies-backsies."

"All I'm saying is, you all can regulate your emotions and keep a level head. Yes, even Jimmy. Sure, it took a bit to coerce him to give up the gun. But he was willing to make a trade for it in the form of a little tit for tat. But Mitch, well, I hate to say it, but he probably would have let his emotions get the better of him and Travis would be dead."

"Why am I always the one being un-alived in these scenarios?" I asked.

Megan leaned into me and whispered into my ear, "Because, sweetheart, you're the one that keeps jumping in front of loaded guns."

"Oh, yeah. I forgot about that."

Megan nodded and smiled at me and we turned back to face Billy. We watched him eject the cartridge and rack the slide one more time just to be sure. He even reset the safety in the middle of it all.

"We'll give Mitch fifteen to gather himself, then we stick to yesterday's plan. Find our parents, even if that means we have to search every home in

Woodridge."

Megan stood up and walked over to the corner of the room. "Travis, could I talk to you for a minute?"

I looked at everyone and shrugged then met up with her in the corner of the classroom.

"Woo-woo!" Jimmy hooted.

"Get it!" Paul hollered, cupping his hands around his mouth to amplify his cheer.

"Shut up you dweebs," Sarah said convincingly, putting them in their place.

"Anyway," Megs said, turning away from the chatter going on behind us. "I just wanted to say that I'm worried about you taking so many big risks. Contrary to what everyone says, I do like you, Travis."

My brow furrowed as I pondered who might be saying Megan didn't like me. I assumed it was Mitch telling his sister that I didn't care for her every time I stayed the night at their place, leading to countless sleepovers of being indifferent toward one another. It wasn't that I didn't like her. We just lived in two different worlds. Until now. Now, our worlds collided and Megan was the perfect girlfriend. At least, I thought so anyway.

"So, you're saying this now because... why?"

"Because," she said, bopping me on the nose with a gentle touch of her finger. "I don't want you to do something stupid like jump in front of a gun and get yourself killed on my account."

"I only did that because I care about you."

"Oh, I totally get that. And it's super sweet, Travis. I'm just saying, I want you alive because I want you in my life."

"I want you in my life too," I said. We stared into each other's eyes, and after a long pause, I pointed at her and then myself. "Are we, like, falling in love right now?"

She held up her fingers and gestured just a smidge. "Maybe a little bit? Yeah."

We looked over our shoulders and found the rest of the gang listening in on our conversation.

"What do you think. Should we give them a show?" she asked.

Raising a finger, I turned around to suggest a way we could tease them when Megan leaned in and kissed me without any prior warning.

After a quick smooch, I looked back at everyone and said, "We're ready."

"Ready to run off to Vegas and elope, maybe,"

Jimmy teased.

Sarah leaned in and whispered to Megs, "Did I just hear you use the 'L' word with Travis?"

"Maybe," Megan replied coyly.

"But you literally started dating him like a day ago. Also, if you'd forgotten, you were like, ew, he's too young for me. Now you're dropping the 'L' word?"

"What are you trying to say?" asked Megan.

"I've watched this kid grow up," Sarah said. "I have baby sat him and Melody since they were five years old. All I'm saying is, I don't want to see him get hurt. Because it's clear that he's already falling in love with you."

"So?"

"So, are you going to feel the same way when school starts back up? Are you going to date your nerdy brother's friend and parade him all over the school? Do you still think you'll be homecoming queen when you're dating a freshman?"

"Do you think I'm that shallow?" Megan asked. She felt slightly offended and in their conversation both girl's voices grew in intensity.

"No, Megs. I've known you forever. I know you're not superficial like that. But I don't see what your end game is here."

"I could say the same about you and Billy. Wasn't that a little sudden, given everything that's happened?"

"Okay, sure. I don't deny that. But it's different. It happened naturally. And, I don't know, it just feels right with him."

"Sure, it's different for you. Let me explain how different. First off, you haven't loved Billy since the first time he set foot in your house. You haven't grown up next to Billy, watching him from afar, and finding every little thing he did adorable. You didn't have years of Billy staying at your house and driving you wild because you wanted nothing more than to confess your love for him." Megs pointed at me and then said, "That's Travis for me. Believe it or not, I've harbored a crush on that kid for almost seven years. Is it weird? Yeah. A little bit. But that doesn't mean what I feel is not real. And secondly, nobody is going to tell me who I can and cannot date."

"Wait, you've had a crush on me for seven years?" I asked, my eyes widening with astonishment.

Megan looked at me, her cheeks bright pink with equal parts embarrassment and excitement. "Yes. That's what I've been trying to tell you this whole time. I friggin adore you, Trav."

"Me too. I mean, I've had a crush on you for, like, ever. I just never said anything because Mitch is my friend, and you were his sister, and you're three years older than me, and... well, I thought it would be weird if I said anything let alone acted on it."

"Quick, somebody write all this down," Paul said. "This... right here is America's new love story."

"Oh, shut up!" Megs and I said at the same time. We looked at each other in pleasant surprise, having spoken at the same time.

"Oh, God, help us all," Melody said. "They're starting to sync up."

Without warning, a loud bang slammed into the glass window of the classroom and we all turned to see Mitch standing outside looking in. His hands were bloody and he left bloodied smudges all over the window as he banged on it.

"You guys," he shouted through the glass. "He's still breathing. You gotta help me!"

We ran to the windows and looked down to find that Mitch had fished the soldier out of the dumpster and had him lying by his feet. Lucy, meanwhile, was nowhere to be found.

"Help me get him inside. The nurses office should have enough supplies to stabilize him and then we'll get him to the hospital."

"Holy, geeze," Paul said, pointing at the soldier, whose chest rose and fell with every little breath. "He really is alive."

"Well, heck," Billy said. "We best not let the poor guy suffer." With that, Billy raced to the side-door and dashed outside and began helping Mitch carry the soldier back inside.

"Grab that blanket," Sarah ordered and Paul and Jimmy quickly grabbed one of the blankets from the night before and ran over to the entrance.

Billy and Mitch set the body down on the blanket and then everyone hoisted the soldier up and carried him to the school infirmary.

"I have a bad feeling about this," Paul said.

"Let's just get him stabilized, if we can," Sarah said. "We'll worry about the rest as it comes up."

We all nodded as we carried the man who was bleeding out on the school floor, leaving a trail of blood all the way down the polished cement floors of the hallway.

# 8

# INVASION
## PAR 8: ROCK AND ROLL

BY THE AFTERNOON, WE ALL HAD TAKEN TURNS watching the soldier and monitoring his vitals as Billy and Jimmy raced back to Fort Liberty to get the antibiotics we'd taken from the drugstore the day before.

I stood watch and informed Melody that it might be best if she kept Lucy away from the infirmary for the time being. The last thing we wanted was for Lucy to show up and finish the job.

Megan kept me company for a while but then left with Paul, Mitch, and Sarah to go look for our parents. They'd scour the parts of town that hadn't been demolished in the fighting in the hopes of finding other survivors.

It was a divide and conquer type scenario. And although I was with the soldier alone, I wasn't afraid.

My sister and Lucy were around and all I had to do was scream for help.

At any rate, after we'd bandaged his wounds, we looked around for a vehicle, or a car, so we could take him to the hospital.

Although the phone lines worked, even though half the town's power was out, there was no answer. Either they'd abandoned the place or they were too swamped to deal with phone calls.

Sarah had mentioned she was going to get her parent's car and drive back. That way we'd be able to get the soldier the help he needed. Because Mitch wasn't wrong, the guy was alive. He was breathing—but just barely.

Lucy had done a number on him, but she hadn't pierced any vital organs. Still, there was a lot of bleeding and he needed medical attention asap.

A couple of hours dragged by and then I heard the sound of a car engine. I leapt up and ran out of the nurse's office and down the hall to the side entrance doors down by the gym. Sure enough, Sarah had found her mom's car.

Sarah and Megan flew out of the car and ran to the doors. They were locked from the outside and they began banging on the doors. "Let us in. Quick!"

Luckily, I was already on the scene and I quickly let them in.

"Shut… the… doors…" Megan said between gasps of air as she tried to catch her breath.

I did as asked and Sarah latched them, making sure they locked. "You two get the main entrance. I'll lock the back exit and the gym doors."

"What's going on?" I needed to be caught up, because they were all in a panic and nothing was making sense. "And where is Paul?"

"Paul found his parents at their church. He decided to stay with them," Megs answered. "And Mitch decided to stay with him. But I'll explain everything on the way. Come on!"

We parted ways with Sarah Lewis and ran to the front of the school and began securing the main entrance. As we locked the doors, Megan informed me of everything that had gone down.

"The church is taking in anyone who missed the evacuation buses. We couldn't find any of the other families. Mine, Sarah's, Billy's, and even Jimmy's parents weren't anywhere to be found."

"My mom?" I asked.

"I mean, she might still be working up at the hospital. But Mr. Anders said the military came in helicopters and moved all the patients to Northwest Memorial in Chicago."

"She probably went with them," I said, realizing my mom would care for her patients even if they were being attacked by aliens.

"As for my brother, I think the past few days have been too much for him. He's too innocent and can't cope like the rest of us, so the Anders agreed to watch him for me. At least, until I can find our parents."

"At least he'll be safe," I said.

Megan nodded in agreement and I could see she was thinking the same thing—it was what was best for him. After locking all the doors, Megan looked at me and said, "The aliens have overrun the town. We thought it was smooth sailing until about six blocks back. Then we came across three of those aliens. We lost them by weaving in and out of several blocks and cutting through alleys, but we don't want to take any chances. If there's even the slightest chance that they could follow us here, we need to be ready."

"Copy that," I said, giving Megan a salute. She laughed.

"Don't be a dork." She squinted her eyes at me and then broke into a big, white-toothed grin.

"But I am a dork," I countered.

She then gave me a big hug and said, "Yeah, but you're my dork."

"Um, guys…" Melody's voice said. We looked over to find her standing in the middle of the hall.

"What is it, kiddo?" Megan asked.

"You need to come see this."

She led us down the hall and to a door none of us had ever seen before. Sarah, having finished locking all the doors on the south side of school, was already standing by the door. She opened it and gesture for us to go in. We went inside and were surprised to find it was a stairwell.

Megs, Sarah, and I followed my sister up to the roof of the high school and stepped outside. She led us over to the edge and then pointed toward the ground.

"Look," she said, still pointing at something.

We all inched up to the edge and looked out across the school grounds. Aliens, just like Lucy, had surrounded the entire high school. All of their tails fanned out behind them and they all lit up bright purple with an eerie ultraviolet glow. One of the creature's squawked and then the others did too.

"Oh, my God," Sarah gasped. Her face went white with fear. "There must be fifty or sixty of those things."

"More," Melody said. "I counted eighty-seven."

"Eighty-seven?" I gulped and pinched the bridge of my nose in concentrated contemplation.

"We can't fight that many," Megan said.

"The doors are secured," Sarah said, "but I don't know for how long. If those things want to get in, they're going to find a way."

"Maybe they just want chocolate?" Melody said.

"That's a nice thought," I said. Her opinion wasn't wrong. If feeding treats to one of the aliens had worked, maybe it would work on the others. But that was a BIG maybe. "But, I'd rather not take that chance. Not with that many of them out there."

Sarah paced back and forth on the roof and then turned to us. "The sun is going to go down soon and then those creature's will be in their element. But, they don't like light, and as we all remember they don't like fire."

"You have an idea, don't you?" I asked.

"Well, there's a lot of school desks and tables

made of wood. And we don't need to surround the entire school. We just need to block the entrances with fire."

"Won't they figure out what's going on?" I asked.

"That's where Melody comes in. I saw that Mr. Ostrander left his boombox in coaches office. What I need you to do is go to the gym, grab it, and bring it back up here. Then you crank that dial to eleven and let those aliens experience the best rock and roll we have to share with them."

"I'm on it!" Melody said cheerfully, and then quickly disappear into the school.

"Megan and I will drag as many chairs and tables to the entrances as possible. When the aliens are distracted, we'll open the doors, pile the chairs and tables and make mini bonfires of them."

"Copy that," I said. I was about to salute, but Megan caught my wrist and just held my arm down at my side. She smiled at me and then let my wrist go.

"All right, on three. One, two, three… and break!"

We raced around the school, using the library carts as makeshift dollies, and prepped about a dozen tables for each door. Then, taking positions, I stood in the hallway by the stairwell entrance and waited for

Sarah to give me the signal. Once she did, I shouted up the stairs, "All right, Mel! Hit it!"

Melody stood on the roof with the boombox, and the melodious sounds of classic American rock and roll filled the air. The first song Melody played was "All Along the Watchtower"—the Jimi Hendrix cover, not the Bob Dylan version—which was quite fitting given the circumstances.

I glanced out the windows and watched a brilliant sunset strip of tangerine orange sink low on the horizon while the aliens all looked up at where the sound was coming from, their tails twitching nervously as they listened to those melodious guitar riffs.

"All is green," I hollered, giving Sarah the thumbs up. With my signal received, the girls unlatched the school doors, shoved tables and chairs outside to block the entrances, and then slammed the doors shut and locked them again.

They repeated this process four more times while I ran to the science lab to gather as many flammable chemicals as possible. Mr. Vanden Bos, the chemistry teacher, even had a whole three liter can of lighter fluid. I also found acetone in both the chemistry lab and auto shop. In addition to this, the auto shop had five gallons of regular unleaded gasoline in a red gas-jug.

Once I'd brought all the chemicals up onto the roof, we filled beakers with highly flammable cocktail mixtures and then began to toss them down. The glass shattered against the piles of desks and chairs drawing the attention of the aliens and they hurried over to see what was happening.

Finally, after everything was thoroughly doused, Megan drew out a pack of cigarettes and a lighter. She kissed a cigarette out of the pack and, with a few flicks of the flint wheel, used the lighter to light it.

"You smoke?" I asked.

Megan took the cigarette from her mouth and coughed. "No," she said, "I found Ms. Watterson's smokes. And since we don't have any matches, we'll use these cigarettes to light the fires." She passed the smokes around and we all took one, even Melody.

"Just lightly puff, but don't inhale or you'll get sick," Sarah warned us. "Once the tip is glowing bright orange, toss it over the ledge and light it up."

We all puffed on the cigarettes until the smoke was so thick we could hardly see one another. Melody was the first to emerge from the haze and flick her cigarette into the air. We watched it twirl as if in slow motion as it cut through the air, white smoke trails following it as it sailed over the rooftop and down toward its final destination. Then, the slow-motion reel snapped back to normal speed just as the cigarette made contact and—*fwoosh!* Flames leapt up twenty feet high, the accelerants doing their job.

"Yeeeeah!" Melody cried out enthusiastically as she leaned over the rooftop to watch the fire burn.

With Woodridge High on fire, the aliens snorted and huffed but kept their distance. They didn't want to risk getting burned and, to our relief, our plan seemed to be working.

Knowing that we had maybe thirty or forty minutes of flames, we quickly went to work filling more of the glass beakers from the science lab with volatile chemicals. In that time, we managed to make about a dozen Molotov cocktails. Cocktail being the optimal word here. Because they were mainly chemical powders and other things that probably *shouldn't* be mixed together.

As the fires began to die down, we lit up our Molotov arsenal and pegged any alien daring to get close to the entrance of the school.

"We're not going to last the night," I said. "We'll run out of supplies long before sun up."

Sarah and Megan shared glances and Melody ran into Sarah's embrace and hugged her tightly.

The aliens kept their distance, but they seemed bound and determined to get inside the school. Our ammunition all but depleted, we sat down on the roof and leaned against the edge of the parapet, occasionally craning our necks and looking over the ledge to check to see whether the aliens had stirred.

Megs checked on the aliens and I asked, "Still there?"

"Yup. Still there," she replied.

"I'm telling you guys, they probably want chocolate."

Sarah let out a long sigh and then looked out at the aliens. "I wonder what they want? They're not attacking us but merely holding a perimeter."

"Maybe they're looking for Lucy?" I asked.

"No," Melody said. "Lucy ran off after Billy and Jimmy left."

Then, Sarah asked a good question. "Why are they just standing out there?"

"Maybe their orders are to kill all humans," Megan suggested. "And they're just waiting to starve us out."

"Alien Siege," I chuckled. "Sounds like a title for a corny pulp sci-fi novel."

"Galaxy Under Siege," Megan said, fanning her hands across the starry night sky.

"There's my nerdy girl," Sarah chirped, throwing an arm around Megan's neck and giving her an affectionate squeeze.

We laughed for a minute and then all fell silent. We sat staring up at the frothy Milky Way sky. A canopy of stellar dust, planets, and stars swirling all about us. How little we all felt compared to the vastness of the universe.

"I wonder where they come from," Melody said aloud. We all nodded.

"I wonder what they eat. Besides chocolate, I mean." I looked at Melody who nodded along.

Picking up my pipe—my weapon of choice—I strolled over to the rooftop hutch that led back into the school. "I gotta pee, you guys. I'll be back in a jiffy."

I opened the door and turned around only to nearly run into the back of one of the alien creatures.

It had somehow found its way inside the school. When it heard the door open, it tried to turn around but the stairwell was too narrow, so it got wedged in sideways.

I slammed the door shut and used my metal pipe to jam the handle shut and prevent the door from being opened from the inside.

"Uh, guys," I said turning around. "We have a big problem."

Sarah and Megan sprang to their feet and looked down over the parapet at the aliens. That's when a loud thump struck the door, startling us all as we spun around to see the door rattle and shake with each blow.

Another loud clank caused us to draw back in fright as the creature tried to batter down the door. Even though the creature was strong, it couldn't get a good run at the door being wedged in the narrow stairwell, so it just banged angrily on door.

Dents formed on our side of the door as it continued to ram it from the other side, but my metal pipe held firm. *Thank goodness.* I looked back at the girls and said, "We're completely surrounded."

Stuck on the roof of the high school with no way

off was bad enough, but to make matters worse, I still really had to pee. As I looked at Sarah, Megan, and Melody's faces, I knew we were all thinking the same thing. This was going to be a crap night.

In the distance, the aliens squawked angrily and it was only a matter of time before all the fires we'd lit died out and then there'd be nothing preventing the whole lot of them from storming the school.

As bad as we had it, though, I only hoped that Billy and Jimmy were having better luck than we were.

I turned and looked to Fort Liberty, but the town blackout had rendered things too black to see.

"What are you thinking?" asked Megan, taking my hand.

"Just that Billy and Jimmy are probably on there way back now. And I really don't want them to find our dead bodies when they get here."

"Don't worry," Megan assured me, "they won't."

"How can you be so sure?"

"Because you have me to protect you." She grabbed her hockey stick and pushed me behind her.

Sarah, drawing out the crossbow that Billy had given her locked in a new bolt and drew up beside us.

"Megs is right. We'll find a way to get through this."

Melody stepped forward and drew a Kit-Kat out of her backpack and peeled the wrapper. Tossing it next to the door, she turned to find us all looking at her.

"What?" she asked. "It's at least worth a shot."

We shrugged and nodded. She was right. We were out of options and anything was worth a shot at this stage. Hopefully, the chocolate would distract it long enough for us to leap off the side of the building and into the trees. Because, at the moment, that seemed like our only escape strategy.

Sarah and Megan squared up in front of the door and I looked around. Melody had found an air shaft that led into the schools ventilation system. Prying off the panel, she said, "Guys, over here."

We all looked back to see her crawl into the vent. Sarah, Megs, and I shared confused looks and then Melodies head popped out of the vent and asked, "Are you guys coming, or what?"

# INVASION
## EPILOGUE

THREE DAYS AFTER THE INVASION... WE KNEW little to nothing about our alien visitors. Before the new agencies got knocked off the airwaves, the latest estimates were that maybe a hundred thousand of the creatures had fallen to Earth from outer space. Where they hailed from, quite literally speaking, and what their purpose might be was anybody's guess.

Woodridge High School was our last standout. It had lent us the supplies and materials we needed to mount a defensive position. And we had held onto it for as long as we could. Which is why it was sad to watch it burn.

It's funny to think. An hour ago, we were trapped on the roof. But then the darndest thing happened. The soldier woke up and, in a state of delirium, wondered out of the school and onto the tennis courts where half a dozen of the creatures mauled him to death. This time, not waiting for our say so. Half the creatures ran off after that. The other half found their way into the school.

With six aliens inside the school hunting us, we decided to sneak back inside through one of the airducts. Now, most airducts aren't like how you see in the movies, unless the building is huge. Like an industrial complex, or, well, a school.

We managed to slide down the airduct and come out into the boiler room of the school. Once inside, Sarah had the idea of setting the boiler to explode. We used the remainder of the chemicals to give the boiler an accelerant to help it burn down the building—along with all the creatures inside.

Meanwhile, the rest of the evening we spent sneaking around the school and locking all the doors in order to confine the aliens to the main corridor. The same corridor that would be the first to get destroyed in the blast.

Melody carried the boombox around on the outside of the building, turning it on to get the aliens to come to her location and then quickly turning it off again before running away to repeat the whole exercise all over again.

It was a modified version of the game "Ding-dong Ditch." A prank that my friends and I played on countless neighbors throughout our middle school years. Looking back now, a prank like that seemed quaint. But it worked well enough as a distraction for these extraterrestrial creatures.

Since the aliens were inside, they only ever ran up to the windows before looking outside and acting puzzled when nothing was there. Then they'd be led to the other side of the school. This game of tag went on for nearly forty-five minutes when Sarah cracked open the boiler room door and peaked outside.

We had finished rigging everything to blow and all that was left was to escape undetected.

"Is the close clear?" I asked.

She held up a hand and Megan and I stayed back. Then, she motioned for us to follow and we all slipped out of the doors into the hallway. We could hear the aliens shuffling about at the other end of the school, and instead of unblocking the entrances, we snuck into the school counselor Mr. Eckhart's office, cracked open the window, and slipped through it.

Once outside, we looked at one another and then

waited for my sister to come running around the corner. We waved her over to us and she nodded and then set the boombox down in front of the main entrance and turned it all the way up.

Racing around to the side of the school, where we waited for her, she huffed and puffed. "I've never done so much running in my life."

"Ka-ka!" a voice said from the trees.

"What was that?" Megan asked.

I put my hands to my mouth and replied, "Kaaa-kaaa!"

"Stop that," Megan said, slapping my hands away from my mouth.

"It's just Billy and Jimmy," I said. "That's our call." I waved them over and they darted out of the bushes and joined us.

"We got the meds," Jimmy said, holding up a bag.

"We won't be needing them anymore," I said.

"Why, what happened?" asked Billy.

"He woke up," Sarah said, "and, well, he went outside and a horde of aliens tore him to shreds."

"Why are we all whispering?" Jimmy asked, still whispering as he looked all around the naturally formed huddle we all shared.

"Because" Melody said tersely, "there are six of those things trapped inside the school and we don't want them to know we're out here."

"Also, we should probably get moving," Megan interjected, "you know, since this place is going to blow."

"What?" Jimmy asked, his ears perking up with interest. "What do you mean it's going to blow?"

"We set the boiler to explode," I said.

"Oh, rad," Jimmy said. "I've always wanted to blow up a school."

"Of course you have," Billy whispered. "It's your whole brand."

"It really is," Jimmy replied. His freckled face lit up with the biggest grin we'd seen from him and he nodded eagerly, anticipating the glorious destruction.

"My car is over by the East side doors," Sarah informed. "If we can all get there, we'll be home free."

With everyone on the same page, we crept along the edge of the school, making sure to stay below the windows and out of site of the hunter-killer aliens.

A few minutes later, we piled into Sarah's old 1981 Honda Accord LX. It was a family four-door and an ugly tan color, but she insisted the manufacturer had called it ivory. Regardless, the important thing was that, like any 80's Japanese car, it was punchy.

Sarah put the key in, twisted the ignition, and the engine came to life. With the wine of the 1.8 liter four-cylinder, high-revving engine, she shifted into first and we tore away from the school.

As the tires squealed, the aliens ran to the windows in time to see two red taillights leaving the school grounds. Everyone but Sarah, who was driving, turned to see if the aliens would burst through the glass and keep chasing us, but they treated the windows as a natural barrier and were, fortunately, contained.

Just as we crossed the threshold of the school gates, the school exploded behind us, taking the trapped aliens along with it.

Unintentionally, the gas main that fed the school also went off and multiple explosions erupted as the main caught fire.

At the same time, a giant ball of flame bubbled up into a brilliant orange and red plume, expanding away from the building which exploded into debris of brick and mortar.

Not being prepared for the additional

detonations, everyone ducked down, flattening themselves the best they could onto the seats.

The deafening blast caused Sarah's shoulders to tense up and she shrank down in her seat, keeping her eyes just above the steering wheel so she could still see the road.

"That was awesome!" Jimmy exclaimed. He was the first to rise back up and watch the school burn.

"Where are we headed?" Sarah asked as she turned onto the only highway that led out of town.

"Just drive," I said. "For now, just drive."

She nodded in silence and we drove East, away from Woodridge and toward the impending sunrise.

In a few hours, dawn and her golden fingers would rise up at the edge of the world and bring forth a new day. But for now, we did the only thing we could. We drove and, although nobody said it, we all knew—there was no going back.

While we had won this battle, the aliens had taken Woodridge from us. They'd taken our homes. Hell, they'd even split our families apart. More than ever, our future was uncertain. But we had each other, and that's what mattered the most.

Megan, who was sitting in the passenger seat,

twisted around and, leaning on the center console, reached back and took my hand. We smiled at each other.

Billy and Jimmy sat on either side of me, and my sister was wedged halfway between me and Billy when, suddenly she gasped.

"Guys," Melody shouted. "Guys, slow down!"

I knew something was the matter because of the anxiousness in her voice. "What is it?" I asked.

She pointed out the rearview window at Lucy, her pet alien, who was trucking along behind us at a brisk pace.

"Wow," Billy said. "Lucy must be doing fifty-miles per hour right now."

"I'm not stopping," Sarah said. "So, wave goodbye. This might be the last time you see it."

Tears in her eyes, Melody put her hand up and touched the glass. Lucy seemed to intuitively know what was happening and slowed to a trot. Then he came to a stop and sat down in the middle of the road and watched us drive away.

"Don't worry," I said. "Maybe when all this is over you'll see him again."

"No," Melody said. "We have to go our separate

ways now. It's for the better."

Nobody spoke because, the truth was, we all quietly agreed with her. Sitting back in the seat, we made ourselves comfortable and watched the corn fields go by as we embarked upon the next leg of our journey.

# TO BE CONTINUED IN:

# THE LORDS OF SUMMER DOWNFALL

## ABOUT THE AUTHOR

Tristan Vick is a multi-genre author specializing in science fiction, fantasy, and horror, and has also dabbled in mystery and suspense. He graduated from Montana State University with degrees in English Literature and Asian Cultural Studies and speaks fluent Japanese. He lives with his wife and three children in Japan. When he's not commuting on the train or teaching English, he spends his time reading, writing, binge-watching his favorite television shows, and eating sara-udon. In addition to being traditionally published, Tristan Vick continues to self-publish under his imprint, Regolith Publications, LLC, and Regolith Comics. His comic book series, The Astonishing Adventures of Alicia Carter & Robot, has sold over 10,000 copies in its first year of release. His other comic book works include Daughter of Wolves, The Profane, Blood & Chrome, The Viking Berserker Zarna, and Animal Woman.

# ALSO BY TRISTAN VICK

▼ Available Now ▼

### The Resurrection Saga
BITTEN: Resurrection
BITTEN 2: Land of the Rising Dead
BITTEN 3: Kingdom of the Living Dead

### The Valandra Time Cycle
Valandra: The Winds of Time (Book 1)
Valandra: The Dragon Blade (Book 2)
Valandra: The Goddess of War (Book 3)

### The Chronicles of Jegra:
Gladiatrix of the Galaxy (Book 1)
Imperatrix of the Galaxy (Book 2)
Destroyer of Galaxies (Book 3)
Galaxy Under Siege (Book 4)
Galaxy at War (Book 5)
A Song for the Galaxy (Book 6)

### ▼ Other Books ▼

The Profane (Novelization)
The Lords of Summer 1986
The Lords of Summer Downfall

Visit Tristan Vick's author website at:

www.tristanvick.com